For Our Little Handsome Man, Hunter.
We love and miss you everyday.

Andrea—
This is not a book plug,
nor am I asking how to get
a publisher! :) I just
wanted to remind you of the
good side of medicine! ♡

M. Rebecca

"Life is not measured by the number of breaths you take, but by the moments that take your breath away."
~ Anonymous

৵ Christmas Eve ৵

৵ Chapter One ৵

The doorbell rings out on Christmas Eve, signaling the first of our guests to arrive. I hear the footsteps of Jake, our Golden Retriever, and Tucker, our Chocolate Labrador Retriever, pitter-pattering on the hardwood floor as they each try to be the first to the door. Not far behind is Sabrina, our two-year-old daughter, in her bright red Christmas dress complete with sparkling ruby slippers. She twirls around, watching herself in the mirror. I can only wonder how I had given birth to such a little princess. My family loves telling stories of how I disliked wearing anything "girly" – bows, flowers, and sparkles included.

Before opening the door, I sweep Sabrina into my arms and kiss her, careful to avoid my pregnant belly. While doing so, I say, "Merry Christmas, baby."

"Mewwy Cwistmas, Mommy. Open da door!"

I place her down softly on the floor and open the large, wooden door, telling Jake and Tucker to stay. They never do, but it is always worth a try. Standing on the other side are our dear friends, Jonathan and Samantha, holding their three-month-old baby girl who is wearing a lovely blue snowflake-covered dress – the perfect blue to bring out the color in her eyes.

"Angel!" Sabrina screams when she sees the baby. I can only hope she will love her own little sibling as much as she loves Angel. I fold Sam and Jon in my arms and wish them a "Merry Christmas." Jon hands me an apple pie saying, "Wow, with the weather out there, we are lucky to have made it. Thank goodness for my pick-up truck."

"I have always loved a white Christmas, but it does make travel difficult," Xavier, my husband, says from behind me as he walks down the stairs. He looks quite handsome in his maroon tightly fitted sweater and gray dress pants. His goatee is closely trimmed and his blue eyes shine in the glow of the Christmas lights lining the banister. Xavier embraces Jon and Sam while giving Angel a kiss on the forehead. Tucker and Jake welcome our guests as well, succeeding in almost knocking Jonathan over in the process.

"Down, Jakey. Down, Tuck-ew," Sabrina declares, in her most authoritative voice. As usual, they obey. I have yet to figure out why they will only listen to her. Xavier and I might as well be talking to the wall when we try to reprimand our dogs.

While we are showing the Wilsons into the family room, the doorbell rings again. As if we had not just gone through the same motions, Jake and Tucker bound into the foyer, barking in joy. Knowing the pups as I do, I understand this will go on all night until the last of the guests arrive. The dogs love company, and so do I, especially at the holidays.

I open the door, this time finding my sister, her husband, and their clan of triplets. The triplets are three years of age, and full of the energy the age brings with it. While I attempt to hug my sister Jenica, Tucker attacks Brody, one of the three, with kisses. Jenica's light brown hair looks as flawless as ever, cut into a short bob. I know I could never pull off the hairstyle as it would make my head look like a balloon. Jenica, always the professional, is wearing classy linen pants and a black sequined sweater.

Jake is busy pulling on the silver silk dress of Brooke, the second of the triplets. Only the third, Bridget, remains in Tim's arms, avoiding the dog onslaught. Tim always has a way of looking completely overwhelmed, yet calm at the same time. He is wearing a blue button-down shirt, and I do not have the heart to tell him it already has a spot of something on it, likely the product of one of the triplets. I kiss Tim on the cheek and point him in the direction of the family room.

I hear Sabrina's voice over the Christmas music yelling, "Bwody, Bwooke, Bwidget!" Yes, thank you, Jenica, for naming your children in such a way that accentuates my baby's lisp. Of course, it only comes out as perfectly adorable.

Jenica moves toward the seven-foot blue spruce Christmas tree, laying each present out in a neat arrangement. I see my daughter's brown eyes glimmer as she sees one gift wrapped in Barbie Christmas paper. Even she is old enough to realize it is most likely for her. Of course, given Jenica and my obsession with Barbies as little girls, I would not put it past her to wrap my gift in the same paper. Along the same lines, it is difficult to say whether the package wrapped in airplane paper is for Brody or Kyle, my 30-year-old brother. Kyle has loved airplanes since he was a little boy and has pursued that love as an aeronautical engineer and aspiring pilot.

Not far behind Jenica and Tim is Xavier's older sister, Melony. Never one to arrive without an entrance, Melony removes her white, faux-fur coat revealing a low cut, red sequined dress and black patent-leather boots that reach her knees. She kisses me on the cheek while saying, "Pregnancy becomes you, Rose. I am glad I decided to never have children, as I would not have been willing to gain the weight. I am sure the baby loves all the Christmas cookies you have been sneaking!" And, not skipping a beat, turns to Xavier asking, "Can you believe I look this good at my age, X (his nickname since childhood)?"

Xavier glances in my direction with a look of defeat and replies, "Great dress, sis." He offers her a drink and walks her into the family room.

As I make my way behind them, in the aftermath of Melony's exotic perfume, I catch a glimpse of myself in the hall mirror. I do not look bad for six-months pregnant, a practicing pediatrician, and a mother of a two-year-old. Not to toot my own horn, but the green cover-up with the black maternity dress is quite becoming. My dark brown hair hangs just below my shoulders and has a slight wave thanks to a new curling iron I bought myself while Christmas shopping for my family. And, my doctors say I have gained the "ideal amount" of weight. So, there, Melony. While I am lost in my self-assuring thoughts, there is another knock on the door.

This time, it is Xavier's good friend, Gil, and his newest girlfriend, Mindy. Yes, her name is Mindy. She is very sweet and seems to really love Gil, but he met her at a local bar, and her name is Mindy. Let's just say, the boobs fit the name. However, it is Christmas, and I refuse to be judgmental. Wait, I think I just was. Well, I take it back.

Gil, a burly Marine of about Xavier's height, picks me up off my feet, kisses my cheek, and leans down to kiss my belly. I have to say, other than Xavier, he is the only man I will let get away with that. I hug Mindy, reminding myself that my breasts will get bigger later in my pregnancy, the natural way. Oops, being judgmental again. Xavier walks into the foyer, also finding himself lifted off the floor by Gil. Gil hands him a six-pack of Christmas ale and they make their way to the rest of the guests.

While there is a lull in the ringing of the door-bell, I join my friends and family. It is always entertaining to stand back and watch my loved ones interact. I see Melony, who is likely telling a story of the latest man to hit on her at the gym, talking to

Samantha by the Christmas tree. Samantha seems interested, or if nothing else, amused. Xavier and Gil are laughing their loud baritone laughs, with Mindy trying to keep Jake from jumping on her likely expensive, little black dress. "Go Jake," I think, then quickly un-think it. It is Christmas, Rose, seriously.

I suddenly remember something important, interrupting Xavier in the middle of his story. "Honey, we forgot to put out the gifts your parents sent. They are upstairs in our closet. I would do it, but with my fat belly, it would take me a lot longer."

In his perfect husband response, he says, "You are not fat; you are glowing and beautiful. I will get the gifts. We should probably give my parents a call tonight too, so they can talk to Brina."

I know that Xavier's parents would rather be here with us for the holidays, but they decided to move to a condominium community in California earlier this year. I have to say, it has been the ideal change for them. Their condo is a five-minute walk from the beach. Mom Gorman, as I call her, can take her morning walk while looking at the ocean. Dad Gorman can sit on his porch, read the paper, and enjoy the sea breeze. Needless to say, Mom Gorman has already found her close friends who were rich and famous in their younger lives. She loves telling their stories. Dad Gorman ran for "Grand Pumbaa" of the community and won. I never would have expected any less. He loves being the man in charge. So, as I said before, they are completely content in their new life. It is different, not having them here for the holidays, but we already have our tickets to visit them for the New Year.

Xavier runs up the stairs, quick to return with a box full of gifts. He asks, "Can I put the gifts under the tree even though I know you will follow and re-organize to make them look *prettier*?"

"I have no idea what you are talking about," I reply, knowing full well I plan to do just that as soon as he turns around.

The doorbell rings again as Xavier is placing the gifts under the tree. It is my brother Kyle, his girl-friend Prilla, along with my parents. My younger brother rolls his eyes as he hugs me and says in a sarcastic tone, "Merry Christmas."

"Why the eye roll?" I ask Kyle as I kiss Prilla on the cheek.

"It never ends with them. Dad complained the whole way here about the number of gifts. The difference now is that the gifts are for the grandkids. We get screwed."

"Stop complaining, Kyle. Your parents are ador-able. Plus, it is Christmas," Prilla interjects.

Kyle retorts, "This is only your third Christmas with them. Try thirty of them, then get back to me."

"Oh my goodness," says my mother, "you kids do not understand. It is who we are. It is how we show we care."

"We know, Mom," I say as I kiss her and envelop her in a hug. "Dad, stop rolling your eyes and give me a hug."

My dad giggles his all-knowing giggle, and truly smiles the second Brooke, Brody, Bridget, and

Sabrina come running into the hall. It is amazing what grandkids can do. I look at my parents and revel in how young they look, not old enough to be grandparents. My father is wearing a light green dress shirt and tie I bought him for Christmas a few years prior. He could have stepped out of a department store advertisement. His hair may have become more "salt" than "pepper" over the years, and my mother may have been coloring her hair for more time than she would like to admit, but I can only hope I age as seamlessly as they have.

Before heading to my dad hoping to play, the dogs have to give their hairy, slobbery welcome to my mom. She is wearing black pants and a white rhinestone-studded holiday sweater, looking young enough to pass for my sister. My mother may be prim, proper, and a bit of a perfectionist, but she does have a soft spot for our dogs. I know her black pants will be covered in dog hair before the night is over.

While watching my parents play with their grandkids and "granddogs," I notice Prilla's charming coat, hat, and gloves. Her blonde curly hair is elegantly pulled up in a twist at the nape of her neck. I comment, "You are always so trendy, Prilla. Even in the winter, you continue to pull it off. You would probably look just as put-together if you were as fat as I am right now."

"Well, the coat was a gift from Kyle," she replies, winking at my brother, "and, you are pregnant, Rose. That is so different from fat."

I say, "The coat is beautiful; Kyle has good taste. It is from years of training, sitting outside dressing rooms while Jenica and I tried on clothes and prom dresses."

"I say it was worth it," Prilla says, kissing Kyle on the cheek. I see she has to step up on her tiptoes to reach his face. Kyle is almost six-feet tall, compared to Prilla's petite five-foot stature.

"Kyle, you are looking quite stylish yourself. I have noticed an improvement since Prilla has been in your life," I say in reference to his white-collared shirt and khaki pants. It is simple, but classy – the perfect combination for my brother.

"Hey, Xavier, can you help me get the gifts from the car? We almost had to rent a U-Haul to bring them all," my dad says sarcastically, over our conversation.

"I can still hear you," my mom replies, while being dragged into the family room by Sabrina on one hand and Bridget on the other.

The room has filled up quickly, making it feel more like Christmas. I decide to walk into the kitchen to check on dinner. Samantha is quick to follow, asking if I need any help.

"No help, but would love the company," I say.

We step into the kitchen and are overwhelmed with the delicious smells of ham and our family's traditional potato casserole baking in the oven, along with the leftover scents of the Christmas cookies made there earlier in the day. I turn to Sam saying, "I know this time of year is bittersweet for you two. Are you holding up okay?"

She replies, "It is never easy, but I have to say, Angel makes me smile even in my darkest moments. She lives up to her name everyday to say the least."

"Well, we all want you to be happy. You know that, but I also understand if it is not the easiest thing. I still get sad sometimes, more than I like to admit, but then, like you said, something makes me smile. I try to remember that things are good. We are very lucky. It sounds so cliché, but it really is true," I tell her, trying to be comforting.

"Life is funny, but Christmas always makes the world look a little brighter, you know? I smile more than cry these days, and I am grateful for that. But, let's not talk about sad things anymore; it is Christmas Eve. What do you think Xavier bought you this year?" She asks.

"Fat women's clothes?" I joke.

"Shut up. I bet it sparkles knowing him!" She says with a glimmer in her eyes.

I am about to respond with another sarcastic retort, but the doorbell rings. Realizing only one person is missing, and that person is always fashionably late, I know I will find my brother-in-law Jack on the other side of the door.

"Merry Christmas, Rose," Jack says as soon as he sees me. "Where are the poochies?" Yep, Jack loves the dogs. I would like to think he comes to our house as much to see us as to see them, but I have come to realize it is not true. Frankly, if playing with the dogs prevents a blow-up between Melony and him, then it is fine with me. I give him a hug, having a difficult time, given my six-month pregnant belly and his 350 pounds. It is never an easy task, but somehow we make it work. Let me make one thing clear, the weight does not run in the family. Xavier is quite fit, thank you very much. There are noticeable similarities between Xavier and Jack's faces, but they are sometimes difficult to appreciate given the difference in their weights.

"Hey, Jack," Xavier yells from the family room, "come on in!"

Jack walks slowly into the family room just as Jake and Tucker bound through the doggy door from the backyard. "Keep them away from the tree, please," I beg while thinking of an incident from last Christmas that almost caused me to lose my holiday spirit.

"Jack, I hope you left Ruby inside at home with the heater on. You never think of things like that," Melony says. Hmm, "Merry Christmas" probably would have been a better start.

"I did Melony, okay? Worry about your own dog, not mine," Jack counters, a hint of escalation in his voice.

"So, wow, everyone is here!" Jonathan says, quick to save the day, as usual.

"Yes, everyone is here. Welcome and Merry Christmas," comments Xavier. "Please make yourselves at home, as usual." I love when the realtor in him comes out, and I often wonder if others notice it as much as I do. Both our mothers are real estate brokers, so I have more than gotten used to real estate lingo around the house.

As the party gets underway, my parents are busy talking with Samantha, who is holding Angel. My mom lights up whenever Angel makes a sound and my dad even seems smitten with the little blue-eyed baby in her adorable Christmas outfit. Sabrina and Brody, trying not to look obvious, are busy checking out the presents under the tree. Jack is playing tug-of-war with both dogs at the same time. Please, please, not the tree. Brooke and Bridget are fighting over leg-space in Tim's lap while Tim attempts to be part of the adult conversation between Xavier and Gil about the upcoming college football bowl games. Kyle, Prilla, and Jonathan are at the bar pouring drinks, while Jenica and Mindy seem enthralled by whatever Melony is relaying. I overhear Melony saying something about visiting the fire station the day before. That would probably be a good story. Everyone looks so happy, which in turn makes me feel perfectly content.

My eyes drift from my friends and family to the fireplace mantle. Nutcrackers are surrounded by garland lining the shelf, which is lit up with tiny white lights. In this moment, however, I find myself more focused on the two picture frames in the center of the festive trimmings. As always, it is the eyes and the smiles that draw me to them. The angelic little baby boy in his camouflage blanket is grinning into the camera as if he could not be happier. His beautiful blue eyes stare out into the room and I feel he is looking back at me. There is such life in those eyes. Then, there is the striking young woman with her long black hair, in her graduation cap, smiling as if she does not have a care in the world. Her blue eyes are as sparkling as the baby's in the frame beside her.

Christmas always has a way of making me feel more nostalgic, opening up old emotions that have long been buried. I hear the Christmas music, currently playing "O Holy Night," but I am in another place. I start to ponder how one simple life, maybe two, can make a difference. One event or one moment in time can truly change the story of our lives, often for the better. Do not get me wrong; there have been many tears along the way. I often wonder whether I would change the course of events if given the option. It is a difficult question, as I do believe things are exactly as they are meant to be right now. I try not to take things for granted, because it would be disrespectful to the tears shed and the pain endured if I ever did. If it had not been for those two souls, the little baby in his camo and the woman with the raven-black hair, my life would be so very different.

As much as I would love to continue on about the Christmas party and all the festivities, there is so much more to this story. As I stand in our family room, decorated for a holiday celebration, surrounded by those I love, I know in my heart that we are all blessed with angels, and I think I have had at least two very amazing ones in my life.

By sharing this story with you, I can only hope you may learn to appreciate the beautiful eyes and the magical smiles that come into your life everyday. Trust me, they matter more than you could ever imagine...

◈ Four Years Earlier ◈

◈ Chapter Two ◈

It was the evening before my first day of Pediatrics internship. I was sitting at home with Xavier feeling excited and nervous at the same time. I reminisced about my days as a medical student, learning new things and trying to find my place in the world. In medical school, I had been given the chance to work with many intelligent role models in the diverse specialties of medicine. My residents, attending physicians, and fellow medical students opened my eyes to new ideas on a daily basis. With each rotation, I discovered more things I loved about medicine, but in my heart I always wanted to work with children.

I sat on our couch thinking back to the road I had traveled as a medical student, the journey that led me to being a Pediatric intern. On my Internal Medicine rotation, I learned to make a diagnosis and form a treatment plan. I also found out what it meant to be at the bottom of the totem pole -

occasionally walking to the coffee shop to collect refreshments for the team. On my Obstetrics and Gynecology rotation, I realized hormonal women and genital warts were not my life calling. When one of my patients gave birth, I found myself wanting to follow the baby to the nursery instead of worrying about delivering the placenta and stitching up vaginal tears. My third rotation was Pediatrics, and I was in love. I still remember many of the patients under my care. I looked forward to seeing their smiling, and sometimes crying, faces each day. Surgery was an experience. I had tumultuous inter-actions with the surgeons, but I loved the thrill of the specialty. I stitched up stab wounds, held a heart in my hands, and assisted in removing a few gall-bladders. It was fun for six weeks and then, I was able to walk away for good. My favorite times on my Psychiatry rotation were those spent on the Child-Adolescent ward. The kids kept me on my toes each and every day. I knew I wanted to incorporate some parts of psychiatry into my practice as a pediatrician.

I could remember my favorite resident, Antonio, telling me, "You are the kind of girl who will succeed at whatever you choose to do. So, you need to do what you love." He was right. I did well in medical school, and likely would have made the most of any specialty choice. Yet, I ended up exactly where I was meant to be, starting my Pediatrics residency.

That night, I was instructed to call my fellow Pediatric resident to obtain "sign out" on my future patients. I did not know what that meant at the time, but I learned rather quickly. She began rattling off a list of patients, medications, abbreviations for medical terms I did not know, and diagnoses I had never been taught. It was intimidating to say the least, but the resident on the line was reassuring and helpful. I was going to be taking on six patients. Two had been in the hospital for a long time and were extremely complicated. Three were new admissions with common pediatric complaints: an upper respiratory infection, a swollen lymph node in the neck, and a new-onset seizure. The sixth patient caught my attention immediately.

The resident started by saying, "The last patient was admitted today. He is a beautiful baby. You will fall in love with him the moment you see him. However, we are at the beginning of working up his condition and do not know his diagnosis at this point. So, it should be an interesting case from which to learn. Hunter Wilson is a five-month-old little boy who was transferred from an outside hospital for elevated liver labs, jaundice, edema, hypotonia, and poor feeding." She gave the details of his history, and said again in closing, "You will really love this little guy and his parents are fabulous."

I thanked her for the information as I hung up the phone and sat at my desk pondering what I had learned. I was so excited to start my intern year. I could not wait to have my own patients, to present at rounds, and to really have a say in decisions. Yet, after hearing "sign out," I wanted to curl up and go back to being a medical student. It was bound to get easier, but I was a bit more nervous than I had been before the phone call.

Xavier could sense my anxiety and suggested, "Maybe you should reread your medical school application essay. I found it in a box just the other day. I think it might be the inspiration you need for tomorrow."

Xavier proved to be right, as usual. Reading the essay that night, I was reminded of the reasons I followed my dreams to become a pediatrician. I was taken back to the times I had bonded with children in the past. I knew the stress and worry would be worth it. The essay read:

"There are things I have yet to learn about life, but I know that I possess innate gifts that will help me to become an exceptional pediatrician. Through my academic endeavors, I have learned that one of my gifts is an aptitude for medical science. The intellectual stimulation of studying and working in the medical field has inspired me to work diligently toward my goal of becoming a pediatrician. My life experiences have led me to discover that I also possess a gift that allows me to open my heart to children. I have a connection with them that is difficult to explain. I have been told it is in the eyes and the smiles. Children see my eyes and know they have a friend. When I smile, they feel comforted. I consider myself fortunate that I can combine my love of medicine and my connection with children and aspire to be a pediatrician. I truly believe if you are doing what you love, you will never work a day in your life.

I held a summer job at a family practice office while I was in college. We had a patient named David who was born to a heroin-addicted mother. One of the first procedures we performed on David was an HIV test. I had never felt so helpless, and yet I wanted to help so much. I learned that even doctors could not control every situation. Fortunately, the HIV test results were negative. My eyes welled with tears when I realized David had a full life awaiting him. I knew the doctor would do everything in his power to help David stay healthy. I saw David often when he returned to the office. His eyes would light up and he would always smile when he saw me. David strengthened my desire to work with children as a pediatrician. It was in the eyes and the smiles.

I was given the opportunity to be an intern at Walt Disney World during my junior year of college. While checking seat belts at the Dinosaur ride, I noticed a little girl in the back row. She had no hair, and she was wearing a medical mask and a pin that read, "Make A Wish." I knew her wish had been to come to Disney World. I asked if she was afraid. She nodded her head, but I saw in her eyes that she was brave. How could she not be brave when she was fighting for her own life? I said I was engaging a magic shield over the vehicle that would protect them from dinosaurs. I pretended to push some buttons and acted as though I could see the shield over the car. Her eyes grew large. She had gained new confidence. When she finished the ride, I asked her what she thought of the experience. Her eyes lit up and I could sense her smile under the mask. She gave me the thumbs up sign. I felt the tears in my eyes. This was her wish and she felt protected. I knew that as a pediatrician, I would be given the opportunity everyday to make children feel safe and comforted. It was in the eyes and the smiles.

For the past two years, I have been a junior high teacher. Evan was a student of mine who possessed great artistic talent. He had a heart of gold, but teachers simply saw him as a troublemaker and did not give him a chance. He struggled with his studies during the first few months of school. Initially, I was unsure if I could help him, but I was determined not to give up. I sat down with Evan and told him we would work together on missing assignments. He went from fifteen missing assignments in the first quarter to one in the second quarter. He continued to improve in many ways throughout the school year. At the end of the year, his parents gave me a card that simply stated, "What a difference one teacher can make." Evan signed my yearbook and when I read the message, my eyes were wet with tears. It read, "This was a great year. It was better because you were my teacher." I looked up at him and caught his eye. He smiled and looked away. Evan helped me realize that as a pediatrician, I would never give up on anything, especially the life of a child. It was in the eyes and the smiles.

I realize that my life would have been very different without these and the many other children I have had the pleasure of knowing. I see dreams and happiness in the eyes and smiles of children, and I cannot imagine wanting anything more than to help them and to care for them. Throughout my life, I have had the opportunity to positively influence the lives of many children. However, in order to take full advantage of my gifts, I know that I must pursue my dream of becoming a pediatrician. As a pediatrician, I will value every child in my care. I know that there will be hard times, and it will be even tougher because those times will involve a child. But, at all times, I will strive to bring happiness to the lives of my patients. At the end of each day, I will feel fulfilled because I will know that I made a difference. It will be in the eyes and the smiles."

I do not think I realized at the time how those words were a prophecy for my future. Every day I would work with children, sick or well, it would be the eyes and the smiles that would continue to capture me. Whether concerned about having an IV placed or happy to see how much they had grown, the eyes would continue to give my patients away. The glittering of the eyes and the shining of the smiles would keep me going back to work each day. I was going to have bad days, and I was right when I said it would be tougher because the difficult times would involve a child. I would cry too many times to count, but I would also smile. I would come to realize that the glory would not come in the expected places, but it would come exactly where I said it would in my essay. It would come in the eyes and the smiles.

I can remember clearly the moment I walked into the hospital on my first day of internship. My eyes were open wide as I tried to take in my surroundings and learn my way around the hospital. I felt like a fish out of water or a chicken with my head cut off, depending which euphemism is pre-ferred. All I wanted to do was meet my patients. As it turned out, I had a whole lot of other work to do in my short eight-hour day as well. I gave myself a crash course on the computer system, and threw myself into the work. It was how I had managed to learn complicated things in the past, so I made it work in this new situation as well.

I finally had time in the afternoon to go around and introduce myself to my patients and their families. Before making rounds, I decided to read the charts on each of my patients, including Hunter Lee Wilson. Hunter had been having feeding issues since he was a newborn. He was always at the lower end of the growth curve, but he had continued growing to some extent. This was a common concern in many pediatric patients, often with a definable cause. The main worry with Hunter was whether his poor growth was part of some bigger picture, given his other symptoms.

He had elevated liver enzymes meaning his liver was not functioning properly. When a patient's liver is not working to its full potential, levels of certain enzymes go up in the blood. This was what was being seen with Hunter. This elevation could have been caused by any number of issues: viral hepatitis, a genetic problem causing his liver to not function correctly, gallbladder issues, or myriad other problems.

Hunter was also jaundiced. Bilirubin is a component of the blood that is broken down in the liver and sent out in urine and stool, or *pee* and *poo* to pediatricians. The products of bilirubin are the reason *pee* is yellow and *poo* is brown. The breakdown of bilirubin is also the reason a bruise changes color from red to black and blue to yellow. When a patient's liver is not doing well, bilirubin cannot be processed and it backs up in the patient's system. Hence, this causes the yellow color change in the skin.

Hunter had developed significant edema, the simple word for which is swelling. He was mildly swollen in his arms and legs, and dramatically in his belly. One cause of edema is being overloaded with fluids that a patient is unable to clear through urination, usually due to kidney issues. Another is the result of a patient's liver not working. This leads to increased pressure in the blood vessels around the liver that in effect pushes fluid out of the veins. The liver is also the organ where the most important proteins in the body are produced. When the liver is not functioning, the patient has less protein in the bloodstream. Fluid has a way of moving to the area with more protein, so it moves to the spaces around the blood vessels instead of staying in them, and this fluid leads to swelling.

A local pediatrician had noticed Hunter was developing hypotonia a few weeks prior to his hospital admission. Hypotonia refers to decreased tone of the muscles. Hunter had not developed the strength in his neck, leg, or arm muscles that would have been expected at five-months-old. His legs were quite "floppy." Hypotonia can be caused by problems in the central nervous system, or the brain and spinal cord, or further out in the muscles themselves. We did not know yet where Hunter's problem was.

When he first arrived at Children's Hospital, one of the biggest concerns was Hunter's blood sugar. He was having a hard time keeping his glucose, or sugar, levels in the proper range. This was likely also related to his liver issues, as the liver was responsible for producing sugar during the times Hunter was not eating to keep his system in balance. We were considering having to put in a nasogastric tube or a tube from his nose to his stomach, so he could get his formula directly into his stomach to prevent vomiting. The plan, however, was to give him a chance to show what he could eat by mouth first.

So, after perusing the chart, the first patient I visited that afternoon was Hunter Lee Wilson. I felt at ease the moment I caught the eyes of his parents. They both smiled at me from around Hunter's crib. I introduced myself, saying for the first time, "I am Dr. Gorman. I will be the intern taking care of Hunter. But, please, call me Rose."

Hunter's father shook my hand and said, "I am Jonathan, and this is Samantha. We are Hunter's parents."

Samantha was an attractive woman, who looked to be a few years younger than my 28 years. She had long, dark blonde hair pulled back in a ponytail. She was wearing a hooded sweatshirt and jeans, which would be my choice for an outfit as well if I did not have to dress up for work. However, she was also wearing flip-flops on her feet, even given the rainy, cool weather outside. I would later learn she even wore flip-flops in the below-zero tempera- tures and snow of her hometown. Jonathan was slightly shorter than Samantha, and looked to be a few years older. He was also good-looking and fair-skinned like his wife. He was wearing a NASCAR cap, but I guessed his hair was also blonde, given his light features.

After greeting Hunter's parents, I looked down at the adorable blue-eyed boy in the crib. He had blonde hair that came to a perfect point in the middle of his forehead. He won my heart immediately as his eyes glittered. He smiled the most delightful, crooked smile I had ever seen.

In that moment, I reflected on my essay and my gift for bonding with children. Early on in life, I did not realize I had such a connection with kids. Then, people began pointing it out to me. Whether in church when kids would turn around to smile at me or in the grocery store line when a baby's eyes would light up when he or she looked at me, there was something special between the little ones and me. It proved to be the same with Hunter. All I could say was, "Oh my goodness. He is just as perfect as described. It is so nice to meet you, Hunter. I think I might be in love."

Samantha laughed saying, "Uh-oh, Hunter. You might have a new girlfriend."

Jonathan included, "But she is a doctor. Nice work, buddy!"

I said, "Well, I have to be honest. Just the other day, I was eating breakfast at a restaurant and I was smiling at a little boy, likely about two years old, in the booth next to me. Later in my meal, he stood up out of his booth, walked over to my seat, climbed up next to me, and kissed me on the cheek. Then, he smiled, stood up, and went back to his family. So, I guess I might be taken. Oh, and I happen to be married, but I think my husband might have to understand."

Sam replied, "Yeah, but you are going to be seeing Hunter everyday, so he should probably be your boyfriend."

"Sounds like a plan to me. We just won't tell my husband," I said with a smile.

We all laughed, and I knew I liked the family already. I took the time to get more information from them about Hunter's medical history. Then, I examined him. He looked into my eyes the entire time and continuously smiled when I talked to him. As documented, he was noticeably jaundiced, and his belly and legs were swollen. When I examined his legs and arms, I did notice decreased muscle tone and decreased strength. Otherwise, his heart and lungs sounded clear.

Hunter was beginning to doze off, so I decided to leave for the moment. I knew I would be seeing him everyday. Before walking out, Hunter did smile one more time. Samantha said, "Goofy man."

I asked if that was his nickname. She said, "Well, that, and 'handsome man,' and 'naked man,' and 'Squeaker.'"

I said, "Squeaker?"

She responded, "From the moment he was born, he has made a squeaking sound. He squeaks when he is sad and he squeaks when he is happy. But, either way, it is pure Hunter." As if on cue, Hunter smiled and made a little squeaking noise. I could not help but smile along with him. It was one of the cutest things I had ever heard.

I said, "Well, I will stick with Hunter for now. But, I am sure I will use the nicknames as I get to know you all better."

᠙ Chapter Three ᠙

By a week later, Hunter had become my hand-some, little man as well. I called him "Hunter-man," "my Hunter," "naked man" when he was naked, and "Squeaker" when he squeaked. My days were never complete until I saw his little smile. Luckily, we had found a way to improve Hunter's weight gain. It did involve placing a tube in his nose to help him feed. Even though he was not thrilled with the tube, it helped him grow and it kept his blood sugars from dropping too low.

We ran multiple lab tests, including tests of his urine, tests of his stool, tests of his blood, and tests of his spinal fluid. A liver biopsy was even done. Not one of the tests came back with a definitive diagnosis. It felt like everyday I told the Wilsons, "Well, we have ruled something else out; we have just not ruled anything in yet either."

The responses from the Wilsons were always optimistic. I can remember Samantha responding once, "At least we ruled *out* something else!" It was true and I was glad they were trying to keep a positive outlook.

Hunter was a diagnostic dilemma, and to make things more confusing, he continued to improve. He gained weight. His liver labs drifted in the right direction. He no longer appeared yellow. His swelling had gone down to just about normal. His muscles were still weak, but he worked with the physical therapists everyday to try and gain strength. We were so happy he was improving, but my team was not able to completely explain that either.

Every morning as an intern, our team of doctors, medical students, social workers, nutritionists, pharmacists, and other auxiliary staff members rounded on patients. Rounding consisted of visiting the rooms of our patients, presenting the cases and any changes from the day prior, and assembling a plan for the upcoming day and for the future. It was a process that allowed families to interact daily with the people involved in the care of their child. A few weeks into my rotation, some members of my team had still not officially met Hunter. When we rounded on him, we would usually stand outside his door. Samantha and Jonathan would join us, but Hunter would stay in his crib. Then, one day, Hunter was in a very good mood. I asked Jon and Sam if they wanted to bring Hunter to meet the whole team. As soon as my colleagues saw him, there was a round of "Oh my goodness!" and "He is beautiful!"

My response was simply, "I told you so."

Nurses would fight over who took care of Hunter each day. I was lucky because I had the pleasure of taking care of him everyday. On my call nights which consisted of a 30-hour shift every fourth night, I would spend time hanging out with Hunter, Jonathan, and Samantha. We would talk about life, work, and Hunter. Jonathan and Samantha were very different from me, yet we got along fabulously. They talked of deer hunting (hence, the name, Hunter) and watching NASCAR. I talked of eating at chain restaurants and following Notre Dame football. But, somehow, we found things in common. The Wilsons never made me feel out of place when I did not know about hunting, rattlesnakes, or the many other topics foreign to me.

Aunt Geri, the sister of Jonathan's mother, was present for most of Hunter's hospitalization. She lived near Samantha, Jonathan, and Hunter and had become close to Hunter in his then six months of life. Jon's parents were back east, in Pennsylvania, which is where I had grown up. Aunt Geri stood in when Hunter's grandparents were unable to be there. She was such a source of support and love for Jon, Sam, and Hunter during that time. I could get Hunter to smile, but Aunt Geri had a way with him no one else did.

There were mornings I would walk in room 2018 and Jon and Sam would be asleep. Hunter, on the other hand, would be wide-awake in his crib. He would talk to himself and giggle and play with his feet. I loved those moments. It was my "Hunter time." He would smile even broader when I came in the room. His eyes would light up, and my whole day would brighten. That baby boy had such a glow. He melted every person who was lucky enough to meet him. Those mornings, we would often simply watch Mickey Mouse cartoons. I had always loved anything Disney, so it was a special bond between the two of us. I would talk to him and laugh at the characters on the screen. He seemed to think they were funny too, because he would join in and laugh right along with me. I was willing to do anything, just to see him smile.

However, he was not always smiling those days. He hated needles and learned early that only certain nurses were skilled at finding his veins. Poking his heels to check blood glucose levels always led to sad squeaks and tears. When he was upset, he showed it. He had a way of scrunching up his face in the saddest fashion. He would pull his arms and legs up to his chest. However, it would only take minutes for his smile to come back, and the sparkle never left his eyes.

During those weeks, I learned about Hunter's favorite things. He loved anything and everything camouflage. His family told me he had worn a camouflage outfit home from the hospital when he was born. It was the "hunter" in him, I guess. He loved a raccoon stuffed animal he had received from the hospital. It was purple and wore yellow shoes. Hunter would giggle and laugh whenever he saw the little raccoon, named "Doozer." He would reach for Doozer and play with him for long periods of time. Hunter's favorite sleeping position was lying on his back with his arms curled up around his head. Looking at pictures from when he was first born, he would hold his arms that same way.

I found myself spending a good amount of time in the Wilsons' room during Hunter's hospitalization. My team began to realize if they could not find me, they never had to look much farther than room 2018. It was such a happy, relaxing place for me. Sam, Jon, Aunt Geri, and any other visiting family members were welcoming, no matter the time of day. I loved being introduced as "Hunter's Rose." And, even more, I loved the responses, "Oh! You are the Rose we have heard so much about."

As the month progressed, Hunter continued to do better from a medical standpoint. He no longer had the feeding tube and was eating on his own. The team decided to perform liver and muscle biopsies prior to his discharge. The reason for these biopsies was to determine if Hunter's condition had to do with his mitochondria. Mitochondria are the energy making bodies in the cells. Without mitochondria, there would be no ATP, or adenosine triphosphate. ATP is the fuel with which the cells in our body carry out their functions. So, if mitochondria are damaged, energy stores are diminished. There are many levels of mitochondrial disease, and many different treatment plans available if one is diagnosed. The reason biopsies were obtained from the liver and muscle was because the most mitochondria could be found in those locations, so the yield was anticipated to be better.

On the day prior to Hunter's discharge, he underwent the two biopsies. We hoped we would finally have an answer. Of course, it was not to be an immediate answer, but something for which we would have to wait. He was not a "happy camper" the day of the biopsies. As I mentioned, he disliked getting poked and prodded. We had to keep the IV in his arm overnight in case we needed to give him fluids to keep his sugars up. He did well, and was still eating like a little champ the next morning.

I was relieved he was doing better, but it was hard to say how long it would last. We really did not know why he had gotten better, because we really did not know why he had gotten sick in the first place. I read articles and textbooks at home on my days off, trying to come up with a diagnosis. There were so many possibilities, but Hunter did not seem to fit any one diagnosis perfectly. We knew he was unique and special, but we wanted his medical condition to be simple and something we could treat.

It was difficult for me to say goodbye to the Wilsons on their discharge day. They had been there every single day since I had started my internship. Hunter was my very first patient. It was going to be different coming into work because I would not have them there. On my call nights, I would not have my little blue-eyed boy to keep me company. I would miss my daily conversations with Jon and Sam. I had made two new friends and just like that, it was time to say goodbye. I knew they had to go. Hunter was doing too well to keep him in the hospital. He needed to go home, have family time, and get used to living outside of the hospital. And, Jon and Sam were going stir crazy, to say the least.

Before they were discharged, I gave Jonathan and Samantha hugs. I told them to have me paged if they came back in town for an appointment. When I looked down at Hunter in his crib, I became sad. He was smiling at me and laughing. He did not seem to know we were saying goodbye. I picked him up and held him in my arms and kissed him goodbye. He cried a little, but he was never really one who liked to be held, other than by his mom. I personally thought he was going to miss me. I wished them luck and said, "I know we will figure out what is going on. It might take some patience, but it will happen. I hope it is good news. It has truly been a pleasure taking care of Hunter. I will miss those blue eyes and that adorable smile."

Sam said, "Say goodbye to your girlfriend, goofy man." She asked for my address, saying she had something to send me.

I said, "You don't have to send me anything."

She responded, "It is already in the works, so we have to send it to you!" I gave them my address, and said goodbye one more time. I hoped the next time I saw them that Hunter would still be doing as well.

❦ Chapter Four ❧

During the upcoming months, I never had quite the connection with a family or a patient as I did with the Wilsons and Hunter. Do not get me wrong; I had some amazing kids in my care, but there was something about the Wilsons that was different. I continued to think about Hunter frequently and found out his biopsy results from the doctors who were following him as an outpatient. Unfortunately, the specimens were not sufficient enough to obtain a diagnosis. It looked as though the Wilsons were no closer to finding an answer. I also realized Hunter had not been to clinic or in the hospital. Those were good signs that he was doing well. At least that is what I told myself to keep my hopes high.

One other patient who did win my heart was an 18-month-old girl named Valerie. I met her around the same time I met Hunter and his family. She also had amazing blue eyes and a smile that brightened the room. I had the pleasure of caring for her a majority of my first month of internship. She remained in the hospital long after that time, so I continued to visit her and her family, even when I was not her primary intern.

Valerie had been diagnosed early in her life with ALL, or acute lymphoblastic leukemia. ALL is a type of cancer affecting young children. Valerie had a high risk type of leukemia that was not responding to appropriate chemotherapy regimens. The chemotherapy she received left her with a poor ability to fight infection. Any bacteria or virus to which Valerie was exposed led to the risk of an infection going out of control. Luckily, over the years, advances had been made in the diagnosis and treatment of ALL, including the use of bone marrow transplants.

I initially worked with Valerie when she was suffering from the lasting effects of a lung infection. She had developed such a severe pneumonia before I met her that she had required a prolonged stay in the intensive care unit. However, her little body fought back and she continued to improve each day. The important thing in those days was to prevent Valerie from developing any new infections, while awaiting bone marrow transplant.

It took Valerie some time to warm up to a new person in the hospital, but she and I developed a bond in the time I was her doctor. I loved seeing Valerie's smiling face on my morning rounds. In combination with Hunter, there were plenty of smiles to go around. Valerie became more playful each day and it got to the point that we could not keep her from smiling and laughing. She was definitely a little "girly-girl," as I called her. There was rarely a day she did not have either her fingernails or toenails painted pink or a pink bow in her small amount of hair.

Valerie was scheduled to have a bone marrow transplant from her older sister once she was stable. It was exciting news for the family and everyone was praying the transplant would make a difference. The transplant would give Valerie's body the healthy cells it so badly needed. With the date of her bone marrow transplant approaching, I stopped by Valerie's room to visit. She was sitting in her crib, as playful as ever. She always loved playing with hospital equipment. She would much rather play with a stethoscope than her other toys. I always joked she would be a doctor when she grew up. I wished her luck with the transplant. Her mother, Delia, told me they still had to run a few more tests before the transplant could move forward, but she had faith things would be okay.

I saw Delia in the cafeteria a few days later. She looked tired, so I asked how she was doing. She said, "I am fine. It is Valerie I am worried about."

She went on to tell me Valerie had developed increasing respiratory problems. The doctors thought it was likely a fungal infection that had run rampant in Valerie's lungs. Valerie was in the intensive care unit. My heart fell when I heard. I asked how these new events would impact her prognosis and chance for bone marrow transplant. With tears in her eyes, Delia told me they did not know yet. The doctors had begun preparing her family for the worst possible outcome. She said, "Valerie's lungs may not be strong enough to make it through this."

I visited Valerie in the ICU later that day. She was hooked up to so many machines. I ran into one of my fellow residents who was currently caring for Valerie. When she looked at me, her eyes spoke volumes. I asked, "It is not good, is it?"

She responded, "The team is not hopeful. She is really sick. She will most likely not make it."

I began to cry, but tried to pull it together enough to go in and see the family. I hugged them and touched Valerie's hand. I whispered telling her to stay strong. I gave the family my love and told them I would pray for Valerie. I said I would visit again soon.

I happened to be on call the next day, meaning I had a million things to do. At one point, I had a moment to pause and my pager again buzzed. Kathy, the resident who was caring for Valerie, told me she had taken a turn for the worse that morning and had stopped breathing. Kathy said the machines were unhooked and Valerie was placed in Delia's arms as she passed away. I could not believe it. I was in shock. I had blind hope Valerie would pull through. I ran to the ICU, hoping to find the family still there to give my condolences. By the time I arrived, they were already gone. The nurses had given Valerie a bath and placed her in bed with a pink blanket covering her. I was told I could have some time alone with her.

It was then I realized my time spent in the Anatomy lab as a medical student and my experiences when older patients died had not prepared me for that moment. We were often taught that physicians should not become too emotionally connected to patients. Well, all I can say is, if there were physicians who could stand in a room with a baby who had passed away and not feel any emotion at all, they would not be doctors I would want caring for my child. It was a life-altering experience. I was glad for the way I felt because I knew it meant I was making a connection with my patients. I knew amongst the crazy hours and overwhelming responsibilities that I was human underneath it all; I was still becoming a physician I could be proud to be.

I was standing there, crying, looking over the body of a beautiful baby. I held her cold hand, and I found myself talking to her. I remember saying, "You are such a loved little girl. Your poor lungs just could not take anymore. I wish we could have saved you. I really loved caring for you, Valerie. God bless you, little one." I cried, wishing things could have been different. In that touching moment, my pager went off. I had to head to the emergency room to admit a new patient. A baby had died and my heart was scarred from the experience. As an intern, the hospital pace did not slow down. Life continued to go on, and I was forced to move along with it.

After Valerie passed away, I became more anxious about my patients' conditions. Occasionally, our team would have to transfer patients from the medical floor to the ICU. At those times, I would visit my patients each and every day to make sure they remained stable. I knew my heart was not completely healed from Valerie, and I realized I had never taken the time I needed to process her death the day she passed.

Later that month, I had the pleasure of caring for an eight-year-old boy named Casey. He was a second grader, aspiring to be a star baseball player. When I first met Casey, he presented to the hospital with abdominal swelling and hematuria, or blood in his urine. These symptoms were thought to be caused by a problem with his kidneys. Casey was a charming boy with a wonderful sense of humor. From the moment we first talked, Casey reminded me of my former seventh grade student, Adam, from my days as a teacher. As I walked out of Casey's room after examining him, I was taken back for a moment to my memories of Adam.

Adam was one of those students who always knew how to make me smile. He had the most amazing sense of humor, one more mature than his years. I remember asking his mother and father at a parent-teacher conference how they ever managed to discipline him. I said, "I try to get upset, but then he smiles, and I melt."

His mother responded, "Welcome to our world."

Even though he was my class clown, I loved him. He was a nice boy who truly cared about his class-mates. He would occasionally pull pranks, but more to make everyone laugh than to hurt someone's feelings. For instance, I remember having to practice with my students for the upcoming Christmas pageant. They were scheduled to sing a very catchy Christmas song. Everyday before dis-missal, I would ask them to practice. I ended up learning the words too and sang right along with them. Unbeknownst to me, Adam had made a plan with the other students. We were singing one afternoon and Adam raised his hand. I realized later that was the cue for the students to stop singing, leaving me standing at the front of the room singing by myself.

Immediately, the whole class burst into laughter and Adam applauded. Half of me wanted to reprimand him, but the other half had to laugh. He had a way about him, and his sparkling blue eyes held so much laughter and happiness. I knew I could learn from him about how to have a consistently positive outlook on life.

The week before I graduated from medical school, I received heart-breaking news. Adam, at that time a freshman in college, had been killed. That fateful day, I was walking through the mall and received a call from another former student. She broke the news, saying she thought I would want to know. I was so grateful she had called me, but I was in a state of shock. It had been the first time I had to deal with the death of someone so young.

I made airline reservations the evening I received the terrible news of Adam's death and traveled to the funeral. It was difficult with my medical school schedule, but I made it work. I looked around the church that day, with tears in my eyes, and found myself feeling so proud of the adults "my kids" had become. Of the 35 students from my first class, 32 showed up to the funeral and the other three had family members present because the kids themselves could not get away from college. It was breathtaking to see them together again and supporting each other at such a difficult time.

Adam's family made the decision to donate his organs, as they believed Adam would have wanted. His uncle said so perfectly in the eulogy, "I have always said if everyone in the world had a little bit of Adam in them, the world would be a better place. Well, I am happy to say, that now there are at least five to ten people walking around who literally do." It was a powerful statement. At the funeral reception, I hugged my students, laughed with them about old times, and cried with them about the death of Adam. Through the reception, a slideshow was playing with pictures spanning Adam's life. In each one, his smile lit up the screen and his eyes sparkled with life. I was reminded of how frequently his smile had brightened my day. His smile and his spirit would be missed more than words could say. I was so blessed to be there with my students, and our bond only grew stronger as a result.

Since Casey reminded me of Adam, I had the same immediate connection with my eight-year-old patient. I took care of him each day, and the team believed he would continue to get better. However, Casey took a turn for the worse. He was diagnosed with a severe case of kidney disease, likely caused by a previously untreated case of strep throat. He became very sick very quickly.

When Casey was transferred to the pediatric ICU, or PICU, the kidney doctors were concerned about his prognosis. His heart and lungs were involved and his blood pressures began running dangerously low. When I first went to see him in the

PICU, he was requiring five medications to keep his blood pressure on the very low side of normal. His parents had been told to prepare for the worst. His family was staying strong, but I shared many tears with them in those days. I was worried we were going to lose Casey, as I had already lost my former student, Adam.

With each visit to the PICU, I tried to be hopeful, but with the information I received, even *my* hope began to dwindle. Each time I walked out of his room, I would say "bye" to Casey knowing it very well might be the last time. I continued having thoughts of Valerie. I was so worried I would come to visit and it would be too late.

Then, one day, I visited and Casey was more awake. The PICU doctors had been able to wean him off some of the medications to stabilize his blood pressures. His body was doing a better job of regulating on its own. Dialysis treatments were helping his kidneys to do their job. Each day, there was something else positive about Casey's condition. He was truly a fighter and a miracle. The smiles began to return to his parents' faces. He began opening his eyes when I came in the room, and their blue color was regaining its shimmer.

Time went on, and Casey eventually left the PICU and came back to the medical floor. I was no longer his primary doctor, as I had switched to a different service. However, I continued to run into him in the halls of the fourth floor. He would some-times be out in his wheelchair or practicing his physical therapy, as he had become weak from his stay in the PICU. One day, I could not believe my eyes when I saw Casey walking down the hall with his parents' support. He looked at me and smiled the brightest smile full of all the pride in the world. I said, "Wow, Casey. I am so proud of you!" It was all I could speak before my eyes filled with tears. Casey continued to improve and eventually went home.

I ran into Casey and his family sporadically throughout the rest of my residency when he returned for dialysis to help his kidneys. Each time I saw him, I was amazed at his progress. When he saw me, he would always smile and wave. His blue eyes never hid the spark any eight-year-old boy's should have. Casey was a miracle and one of my happiest stories from intern year. I could only hope the "Casey-like" endings would outweigh the "Valerie-like" endings. I kept praying Hunter was going to be one of the happy ones.

෨෨෨෬෬෬

Each day brought new patients and new chal-lenges, and I did love going to work most mornings. Xavier usually sent me text messages throughout my long days at the hospital. He would send funny ones, for example, "Melony is mad at Jack for telling a guy she likes how old she is! They are not speaking. Typical." He would send text messages about current events, since I was out of the loop at the hospital, for instance, "We elected a new president!" With as much time as I spent at the hospital, I pretty much wrote back, "President of what?" Okay, so it was not that bad. One day, he texted, "You are going to be happy! You received a package from Hunter

Wilson!" I could not wait to get home to see what it was.

I ran in the apartment to open the package. Jake and Tucker, expecting belly rubs the moment I walked through the door, could not figure out why it seemed I was ignoring them when I entered. I opened the box from the Wilsons quickly. Inside, I found an 8x10 picture of Hunter in a purple outfit, his favorite color. He had the cutest smile on his face; it was a little crooked with his tongue sticking out a tiny bit. Also inside, I found something un-expected, something that brought tears to my eyes. The Wilsons had sent me Doozer, the little purple raccoon Hunter loved so much. It had a bit of formula on its ear and it smelled like Hunter, which made it even better. I could not believe they had sent me something so special. I was showing Xavier the picture and Doozer when I noticed the writing on Doozer's tag. It read, "To My Rose. Love, Hunter."

Xavier said, "Hunter is pretty damn cute, Rose. I can see why you love him." I realized this was the first time Xavier was seeing the precious face I had come to adore. I agreed with him, as I hugged Doozer close to my chest. I remember hoping Hunter was doing well and praying I would not see him any time soon in the hospital. It was one of the conundrums of being a physician in a hospital setting. I grew close to my patients during their stays, which made it hard to say "goodbye." I would often say as they left, "As much as I would love to see you again, I do not want to see you back here in the hospital." I could only hope I would bump into them at the grocery story or at a future well child visit. In most cases, saying "goodbye" meant I would not see them again. That was usually a good thing as it signified those children were staying healthy.

ৼ Chapter Five ৼ

As an intern, there was very little "down-time." Yet, when I did find myself sitting on the computer with little to do, I would check the patient rosters of other teams. Since I had been in the hospital for months at that point, I was starting to recognize some of the patients' names. When I found a child I knew, I would try to visit and see how they were doing. One day, I was scouting the lists and was surprised to see "Hunter Wilson" in room 2124. My heart skipped a beat. I was concerned as to why he was back in the hospital.

I found myself walking quickly to his room. As sad as I was to see he was back in the hospital, I could not wait to see that smile and those beautiful blue eyes. When I walked in the room, Samantha and Jonathan both lit up with smiles. Sam said, "Look, Hunter, it's your girlfriend, Rose."

I looked down at him in his crib and he smiled. It absolutely brightened my day. I had almost forgotten how adorable he truly was.

I said, "I am glad I saw you were here, but I am sad you are back. What's going on?"

They explained that Hunter's liver enzymes were slightly elevated again, and the gastro-intestinal, or GI, specialists wanted to repeat his liver biopsy. His team wanted to try and identify a diagnosis. It sounded as if, all things considered, Hunter had been doing well. They told me he was moving his legs more and trying to work on sitting up. I was so proud of him.

I could not stop smiling at the little, handsome man. He had grown so much in only a few months. His hair was longer and more blonde and now curled at the back of his neck. He smiled as if he remembered me. Of course, Sam and Jon said he did, but I think they were trying to make me feel good. They asked if I could be their doctor again. I had to explain that I was now on another team, but I would be there in the hospital everyday and would be sure to still visit.

Jon said, "I am not sure about our new intern. He just came in really quickly and didn't pay that much attention to Hunter. We said, 'We miss Rose.'" Again, I think he was being sweet to me, but it was still nice to hear.

I told them I had received their package and that Doozer, the raccoon, and the picture of Hunter were both residing on my nightstand. I said, "Xavier now realizes why I was cheating on him. He said, 'I would cheat on me too with a little guy that cute.'" Jon and Sam both laughed.

Sam said, "That's right, huh, goofy man?" This of course made Hunter smile.

As usual, I got paged and had to leave the room. I promised to return the next day to check in and see how they were doing.

When I went home that night, I saw Doozer sitting on my nightstand. I wondered whether I should bring it back for Hunter to have while he was in the hospital. However, I convinced myself the Wilsons might take the gesture as my not wanting the gift, which was not true at all. I cherished it. So, instead, I decided to find him another purple stuffed animal, one that could be a gift from me.

I came in the next morning and went directly to the gift shop. I found the cutest purple monkey stuffed animal that made monkey sounds when squeezed. I knew the sounds would make Hunter laugh. I wrote on the tag, "To Hunter. Love, Your Rose."

I brought it to the Wilsons' room. They opened the gift and said they loved it. Hunter was asleep at the time, and they promised to give it to him as soon as he awoke. I asked for the medical update. They said the doctors were going to let them spend the weekend with family, and then they would return on Monday for the biopsy.

I said, "Oh, I was kind of hoping you would be here this weekend, because I need somewhere to watch the Notre Dame game." Since graduating from Notre Dame, one of the hardest parts of internship was working on football Saturdays.

They apologized, but said they would be looking forward to seeing me Monday. I promised I would find them.

The weekend was busy at the hospital. I was able to sneak away to watch parts of the game in the cafeteria, the resident lounge, and occasionally in an empty patient room. Monday rolled around and I was seeing my patients. I glanced in the window of room 2018 – Hunter's old room. I saw the Wilsons sitting in their same spot on the couch. It felt like old times.

I knocked and entered. Sam and Jon were sitting playing with Hunter. He was holding his head up pretty well on his own and was busy playing with his monkey stuffed animal. He smiled when he saw me, and as usual, his little eyes glittered. Sam said, "We named the monkey 'Rose.' Hope you don't mind."

I said, "Don't worry, I am not offended."

Jon squeezed the monkey and it made sounds. It set Hunter off into a fit of giggles. God, it was cute. We talked for a while, catching up on life and other things. They said the nurses were going to have to place an IV and Hunter was not going to be happy. I replied, "Well, then, I might head out while you are still smiling, huh, handsome man?"

The next day was the liver biopsy. As usual, Hunter was a trouper and made it through. The GI doctors wanted to keep him overnight to ensure he remained stable. He maintained his blood sugars, and was ready for discharge.

On the day the Wilsons headed home, I gave them my email address, asking them to write, send me pictures of Hunter, and keep me updated on any news about the biopsy. They promised they would. We hugged goodbye again, hoping the next time we saw each other it would be for a good reason. I kissed Hunter and he smiled. If only I had the ability to truly describe that smile. If I could bottle it up and sell it, I would be a millionaire. His chubby cheeks would lift as the corners of his perfect mouth curled upwards. The right side of his mouth was always a little behind the left, which made for the most precious crooked smile.

Near the end of October, I received my first email from the Wilsons:

"Hi Rose!

This is Hunter, Samantha, and Jonathan. We just wanted to catch up and see how you are doing? We hope you're doing great. So, one reason for the e-mail is to let you know that Hunter said 'Mama!' He was lying in bed, and Jonathan kept saying, "Say Dada, Hunter". I walked right up to him, said, "Say Mama," and sure enough, he said it! Twice in fact! So exciting! Sorry we have not sent any recent pictures, but our Internet isn't very fast. As soon as we get anywhere with decent Internet we will be sure to send you some, and of course, some on Halloween!

We really hope you've been doing great!

Samantha, Hunter, and Jonathan"

The email made my day. I could picture little Hunter turning to Jon, with a smirk on his face, then looking at Sam with his big, blue eyes and saying, "Mama." It must have been a memorable moment for them, well, at least for Samantha. I was so flattered they wanted to share the experience with me as well. I emailed back, thanking them for keeping me up-to-date on Hunter's progress. I promised to stay in touch and awaited the next email, hoping for pictures of Hunter dressed up on Halloween. I was sure he would look as adorable as ever.

ဆ Chapter Six ဆ

During the beginning of November, I spent one rotation at a different hospital, away from Children's. It was hard to be separated from the kids I had grown to know and love. I found myself wanting to visit Children's on my days off to check on my patients. At least I knew I was on the path to a career I would love, seeing as I missed it when I was away for even a few weeks. I knew the hours were long and it was not always easy to care for sick children, but there was nowhere else I wanted to work.

I will never forget the day I received the next email from the Wilsons.

"Hi Rose,

Unfortunately we have some bad news. We were flown in yesterday morning and we are now at Children's in the ICU. We have a diagnosis. He has a mitochondrial enzyme deficiency and so they are working on that. I actually took him to the emergency room on Friday where we live because I couldn't get him to eat and his sugar was dropping. There, he started to eat and it went back up.

The next day he wouldn't sleep, was always crying and we couldn't get him to eat. So, we drove the hour to our local hospital, hoping they would give him an IV, which they didn't. He ate some there and then we were sent to the Ronald McDonald house for the night. After three hours of being there we still couldn't get him to eat or sleep, so we went back to the emergency room where they gave him an IV (after about four hours) and ran blood tests. His liver enzymes and coagulation studies were so bad that he had to be airlifted which was fine by us.

I hope your work has been okay! If you get some extra time, be sure to come by and see us. We know Hunter would love to see you!

Talk to you later,

Hunter, Samantha, and Jonathan."

My heart sank to my stomach as I read the email. A mitochondrial enzyme deficiency could mean many things, so I wanted more information. I was worried about Hunter. I knew if they flew him to Children's and he was in the pediatric intensive care unit, or PICU, he was very sick. My eyes filled with tears when I thought of how frightened Jon and Sam must have been. I wanted to get in the car and drive right then, but I was on call for the other hospital.

Sam had said his liver enzymes and coagulation studies were elevated again. The liver is responsible for making some of the factors involved in the coagulation cascade. If a patient's liver is not functioning, those factors are not made, and the blood has a hard time clotting. In those cases, if the patient were to start bleeding, it would be very difficult to stop. It was an incredibly high-risk situation. I knew Hunter was in good hands and believed in the ICU doctors caring for him.

Before heading to sleep that night, I emailed the Wilsons.

"Oh my goodness! I am so sad to hear all of that has happened. I know Hunter is in good hands in the PICU. The doctors are fabulous and brilliant. I am not working at Children's right now, but I will try to stop by this week, most likely on Thursday. Please email me if anything changes or if you need anything. I know this is all scary right now, but Hunter is very strong. We all know that. He is a little fighter. Give him a kiss for me, please. I will see you all soon. Let me know if you need anything, otherwise, see you Thursday.

Love, Rose."

It was difficult to wait until Thursday to visit Hunter. I heard he was moved from the PICU to the medical floor the next day and figured that had to be good news. His labs were likely still elevated, so it was going to be a long road, but at least he was stable enough to be out of the ICU.

That Thursday, my residency classes were cancelled and I took the opportunity to visit Hunter and his family. When I walked in the room, there was a sense of sadness. As usual, Jon and Sam smiled when they saw me, but there was something in their eyes, something that caused my own eyes to fill with tears. Hunter's Aunt Geri, the one I had met back in June, was also there at Hunter's crib-side. I hugged them and asked how things were going. Sam began to cry as she explained, "We have the definitive diagnosis. It is mitochondrial DNA depletion syndrome. It is not good, Rose. There could be a chance for a liver transplant, but they do not even think that would make much of a difference. We are waiting for the brain MRI results to see about his prognosis."

I was at a loss for words, which rarely happened. I did not expect to hear such terrible news when I arrived. I looked down in the crib at the sleeping, adorable boy. He did appear a bit yellow with jaundice and slightly swollen, but not much different from the first time I had seen him. I said, "I am so sorry. I do not even know what to say. So, are they going to have a meeting with you to discuss things?"

Jon said, "Yeah, tomorrow afternoon once they have the MRI results. Are you going to be there?"

I apologized, saying, "I wish I could be, but I have to work at another hospital tomorrow and will not be back at Children's until next week. I know the team here will take good care of you."

"We know. We did not know if you would be here, too," Jon replied.

"No, unfortunately not. And, I would stop by this weekend, but Xavier and I are going to be out of town. If I had known all this would happen, I never would have planned the trip," I said, feeling terrible.

"Don't be silly, Rose," Samantha said. "You need your vacation. You already work too hard. Where are you going?"

I replied, "Well, Saturday is my birthday, so Xavier is taking me to Disneyland. But, part of me would rather be here with you guys."

Of course, in a way only the Wilsons could, they put aside their problems for a moment and were excited for me. Sam said, "Wow, Hunter-man, Rose gets to go to Disneyland. Better wish her a happy birthday!" I was always blown away by how easily they could be happy for someone else. It was a true gift.

Hunter opened his eyes for a few minutes while I was in the room. I whispered to him, "All I want for my birthday is for you to have a good weekend and to keep doing okay. Can you do that, handsome man?"

I think I caught a sparkle in his eyes. Aunt Geri turned to me and asked, "If I would give him part of my liver, would they let us do the transplant even if he wasn't the ideal candidate?"

I did not know the answer to that question. So, I said, "I do not know all the intricacies of the transplant process. Be sure to ask all your questions during the meeting tomorrow. Trust me, everybody knows how loved this little guy is. We will give him every opportunity. If it came down to it, I would even give part of my liver. That is how special he is. But, it is really the people in the meeting tomorrow who will be the best to answer your questions. I wish I could be there."

Jon said, "No, you need to go have fun on your birthday. We will still be here when you get back."

I responded, "Actually, I do have some good news. At least, I hope it is good news. I will be coming back on the GI service starting next Wednesday. So, I will be requesting to be Hunter's doctor again if that is okay with all of you."

Sam said, "Okay? We would request you, too! That makes us so happy that you will be back. We cannot wait, huh, goofy man?"

Hunter looked at me in some type of agreement. I noticed Rose, the monkey, was still close-by in his crib, watching over him even while I was not there. I said "goodbye", reminding them I would be back for good on the following Wednesday.

৯৹৯৹৯৶৶৶

Xavier and I had a memorable weekend in Southern California, including a fun day in Disney-land on my birthday if I could overlook Notre Dame's pathetic loss to Boston College. However, I still found myself thinking and worrying about Hunter. On the night we returned home, given I would be taking over Hunter's care on Wednesday, I checked his chart in the hospital computer system. I found a note from the Palliative Care service, a won-derful resource for families. The team was called when a patient's condition was unlikely to result in long-term survival and when a family would need help with difficult decisions about the care of their child.

There had been a conference held on the day before my birthday with the Wilson family. The liver doctors and the rest of the team discussed Hunter's diagnosis of mitochondrial DNA depletion syndrome with the family. Unfortunately, according to the notes, his prognosis was quite poor. Given the involvement in Hunter's brain seen on MRI, the neurologists felt he was not a candidate for liver transplantation. This was difficult for the Wilsons to accept. They asked the right questions, but the doctors explained he would likely not develop beyond his current neurological state. His body may not even survive the transplant, and with his labs and his diagnosis, the transplant would not be curative. By the end of the conference, there were many tears, but Samantha and Jonathan had decided to make Hunter "comfort care only."

"Comfort care" meant everything done from that point would be done simply to make Hunter comfortable. Sam and Jon had the reins. If they changed their minds at any point or wanted anything done at any time, they had the green light to do so. However, they made it clear they did not want to do anything that would prolong Hunter's suffering. They also did not want to institute treatments that would then need to be discontinued; they did not want to have to "pull the plug," so to speak.

I read the notes from the conference, and I cried. I am usually quite a pessimist when it comes to my own life, but an optimist about my patients and family members. I still wanted to believe there was hope for Hunter. After seeing the MRI and reading the consultant notes, from a medical standpoint, I finally had to come to grips with the idea that Hunter was going to die. Nobody knew how long it would be, but the consensus was it would happen. This was very hard for me to get my mind around. I could not believe that only a little over four months after I had met Hunter and his family he was dying. If anyone had told me in June this was going to happen, I never would have believed it. Hunter was too beautiful and too precious, but I guess those things did not always matter. I was never going to give up hope in a miracle, but my brain kept telling me the other doctors were right, and Hunter was not going to make it. I think that was the first time I had to deal with the definitive fact a baby was going to die, and not just any baby, but our little, handsome man.

Since I was already on my computer, I began searching for "mitochondrial DNA depletion syndrome." I had some idea of what it was, but since it was very rare, I did not know the specifics. Unfortunately, the information I found was not reassuring. Hunter's liver biopsy results showed he had less than 5% of the normal amount of mitochondria, or less than 5% of the energy-making parts of his cells. His brain and liver were at most risk with this condition, as those are the organs that require the largest amounts of mitochondria to function adequately. It was amazing Hunter was even doing what he was doing – playing, saying "mama," smiling, laughing – with as little energy as he would be able to produce.

The worst part of all was most of what I read said babies with Hunter's diagnosis did not live past 11 or 12 months of age, and Hunter was already 10-months-old. The information seemed to say there was little to do for these infants. Some children with this condition had higher percentages of mitochondria than Hunter, but still less than what would be considered "normal range." These children had a better chance, but still a shortened life expectancy. Babies like Hunter, with less than 5% of the normal number of mitochondria, had very poor prognoses.

With the additional brain involvement seen on MRI, the prognosis was even worse.

I wondered if the first liver specimen had been adequate and we had diagnosed Hunter earlier whether that would have changed his prognosis. From all I read on his condition online and in the notes from his various providers, it would not have changed the outcome. His numbers were so severe, and would have been equally as severe back in July. So, unfortunately, it felt our hands were tied. I had always wanted to be able to give the Wilsons a diagnosis, and now I wished we were wrong. Unfortunately, I knew we were right.

I also read in the notes that Sam and Jon requested Hunter be in the hospital until he passed away. They wanted to be on the medical floor, not in the ICU. They knew the nurses and the doctors and felt the most comfortable there. It was not a common request, but it was one that would be respected and carried out. That meant I would most likely be Hunter's doctor when he passed away. I was more-or-less his first intern at Children's Hospital and I would probably be his last.

That night, I knew I still had to get through two more days on my other rotation. All I wanted to do was return to Children's so I could be there with the Wilsons. I busied myself over the next two days with work trying not to be overwhelmed with Hunter's situation.

The night before going back to Children's, I received a call from Catherine, Hunter's current intern. She wanted to give me "sign out" on everything that had transpired. The first thing she said to me was, "Wow, you must really have good rapport with this family. They requested you. Even with everything going on, they are so excited you are coming back to be their doctor. They have been asking when you would be back for days now."

I replied, "Yeah, well, they are quite special to me too. I am glad I am coming back, but I am sad about the circumstances."

She ran through the medical information – what medications he was still taking, how he was being fed, what we were able to do for him, and what his parents had requested we not do. She iterated that, all in all, he was struggling along, but it could change at the drop of a hat. I asked how he looked. She replied, "Not too good. You should be prepared for that."

Thanking her for the information, I hung up the phone and thought back to that night four and a half months ago, the night when I received sign out on the new little five-month-old who had been admitted. I could remember thinking we would find a diagnosis, so full of hope and all the good intentions that came along with being an intern on the first day of internship. In a way, it was difficult to shake the feeling that we had failed Hunter in some way. I had read about his diagnosis and knew it was fatal, but it was difficult to let go of the notion that I should have done more. I would come to realize down the line, sometimes it is not a matter of diagnosing or treating; sometimes it is simply a matter of being there.

ာ Chapter Seven ာ

It was difficult coming back to Children's with the knowledge of Hunter's prognosis. The Wilsons had learned heart-breaking information since I had seen them last. I did not know how their spirits would be holding up, but at the same time, I wanted to be there. I could not imagine it any other way.

I was sitting in the residents' room on my first morning back at Children's Hospital, and Natalie, Hunter's nurse, entered. She said, "Oh good Rose, you are back. The Wilsons have been asking about you for days now. They wanted me to tell you they left something on the table in their room for you. Be sure to pick it up."

I thanked her and began my morning rounds. I walked into room 2026, Hunter's room. He was lying comfortably in his crib with his camouflage blanket and Rose, the monkey. He looked as perfect as ever. I examined him without waking Sam and Jon who were asleep on the bed. Hunter's heart and lungs sounded stable, but his belly swelling, or ascites, was worse than I had seen it in the past. Before leaving, I noticed a card with my name on it sitting on his crib-side table. I took it with me when I left.

I opened the card with tears catching in my throat. It said, "Dear Rose, You have a special place in my heart! Happy Birthday. We hope you had a great time in Disneyland! Love, Hunter, Samantha, and Jonathan."

As always, the Wilsons proved to be selfless. They had the terrible meeting the previous Friday, a rough weekend with all the decision-making, and yet, they thought enough to buy me a birthday card. It really touched my heart. There were not words to describe how honored I was. These were remarkable people who were losing their precious boy. I only hoped I could be half the gift to them they had already been to me.

I came back later in the morning when Sam and Jon were awake to say "hello" and tell them how sorry I was about the news. I walked in the room and their eyes gave them away. There had been many tears since the last time I had seen them. All I could say was, "I am so sorry, you guys."

We exchanged hugs as I leaned in to say "hello" to Hunter who was asleep in the crib. I asked Sam how she was holding up. She said, "We have done a whole lot of crying, but with family support, we are slowly coming to grips with things. We are trying to keep our spirits up to enjoy Hunter as much as possible."

"Well, then, you are doing the right thing. I am here now if you need anything. Please do not hesitate to ask," I replied.

"My family cannot wait to meet you. My parents and grandparents are here and they have heard so much about you," Jon said.

"I cannot wait to meet them either. And, thank you for the birthday card. You did not need to do that. It was so sweet. My birthday was nice, but I have to say, I thought about Hunter all weekend."

"Well, we wish you had been here for the meeting and everything, but we were glad you were off enjoying yourself too. We were joking that we should have taken Hunter out of the hospital and snuck him to Disneyland with you," Sam said with a smile.

At that, Hunter opened his eyes. "Oh, hey, Hunter-man. I would be honored to take you to Disneyland. You would love it, since I know how much you adore Mickey Mouse," I said.

Jon's Aunt Geri was back again and as sweet as ever. She loved telling me stories about Hunter and she always had a way of including me in conversations. She pulled me aside on my first day back and said, "Rose, be honest with me. We need to be preparing Jon and Sam for what is coming. Do you have any idea how long we have with him?"

I replied, "Geri, you know I wish I had the answer to that, but I don't. With each day that passes, I can try to give you more of an idea, but we know Hunter. He has a way of having a bad day and then bouncing back for a good day the next. It is going to be a rough road, but let's just hope the good days outweigh the bad and take it one day at a time, okay?"

She said, "Okay, thank you. We are all glad you are back."

During those first few days, I was already starting to feel like one of the Wilson family. Believe me, it was an incredible family of which to be a member. They reminded me in many ways of my own family. Maybe it was the Pennsylvania connection or maybe it was the "good people" connection; it was hard to say. The family even moved their camper into the hospital parking lot, a move that included bringing along a grill and room to cook dinner.

Sandy and Vince, Jon's parents, became the honorary cooks. They were so sweet to me from the day we met. We developed a very close relationship, and they too have become like family. Vince loved to cook and it showed. He never made a meal without inviting me to join them. He said, "If you have to be here, you should be able to eat well. It is my way of saying thank you." After months at the hospital, I had to admit, I was sick of cafeteria food. I hated to accept food from my patients, but Vince would not take no for an answer. One time, he even barbecued elk. Vince asked, "So, Rose, do you like elk?"

I responded, "Umm, you ask that as if I may have actually tried elk before." The Wilsons laughed. They seemed to always get a kick out of how much of a "city girl" I was.

They said, "Try the elk. Do it for Hunter." I could not say "no" to that. So, I tried it. And, I have to say; it was quite tasty. I even had more than one bite.

Hunter's great-grandparents, Nanny and Poppy, were also there and I grew to love them both. They were the prototypical great-grandparents. They could make me laugh, but they were so sad about Hunter they could also make me cry. When either of their eyes connected with Hunter's, there was a spark that could not be ignored. They loved their great-grandson more than anything. They both started taking care of me in the same way they cared for their own grandchildren. They made sure I was eating and sleeping well and included me in family discussions. I could tell how heart-broken they were about Hunter, yet they stayed strong for their family.

❦❦❦❦❦❦❦

My second night back as Hunter's doctor, I got a page from his nurse, Natalie. When I called back, she said, "Hunter just had a funny episode and now he is breathing in gasps. Can you take a look at him?" I told her I was on my way.

As I walked to his room, I was selfishly thinking, "God, please. Not right now. I am not ready."

When I walked in the room, Sam's eyes caught mine and I knew she was concerned. She was holding Hunter in her arms and I could hear him breathing from the doorway. Geri said, "He was lying on the bed, then he looked like he was going to vomit. We ran over and tried to pick him up, but he had already started."

Sam jumped in, "Yeah, we picked him up, but I am worried he may have already gotten some in his lungs. He has been breathing funny ever since. And, we had just given him formula through the tube in his nose about five minutes before." Hunter was using the nasogastric tube, from his nose to his stomach, to help him eat, as he had on his previous admission.

"Let me listen to him," I said. I listened carefully to his lungs. He was moving air well and there was not a focal area that sounded different than the others. It sounded like he had phlegm or formula sitting in his upper airway.

I told the Wilsons what I heard. I explained, "Well, the one thing we could do is suction him a little deeper to try to clear all that phlegm out. I know it might be a bit more invasive than you would want, and I know he will most likely not like the process. But, overall, I think it will make him more comfortable if he can breathe easier. How does that sound to you?"

"Yes, we agree," Sam replied for the both of them.

"Okay, let's do it, then," I concluded.

The nurse suctioned him and did not clear much out, but it seemed to help Hunter cough a little. He started breathing easier and his breath sounds were quieter than when I first walked in the room. The family felt much better, yet I knew the episode was quite a scare. They were appropriately concerned that he might keep vomiting. I told them we could always give him the fluids and sugars he needed through an IV and take the tube out of his nose. Although he would not be receiving some of the nutrients from the formula, he could still get the most important things his body needed through the IV. They agreed to consider the option.

As the days passed, I met more of Hunter's uncles, aunts, and cousins, all of whom took me in as their own. It never mattered who was in the room when I entered; I was welcomed at any time. I even walked in while they were having family pictures taken by a photographer. This gentleman came to Children's Hospital and took black and white photos of families with children who were dying. It was still hard to believe Hunter fell into that category. The pictures were compiled into albums as keepsakes for the families.

I waved and said I would be back after the photos were done. Sam and Jon said, "No!"

Sam said to the photographer, "This is Hunter's doctor and we want her to have pictures with him, too."

I was honored, so I agreed to stay. The whole family posed with Hunter and he looked absolutely handsome. He was wearing camouflage pants, of course. When my turn came, I took Hunter in my arms. He cried a little at first, but once he was comfortable, he snuggled against my shoulder. My heart broke slightly as I felt him breathing against my chest. We took a few pictures and I knew, in that moment, I would cherish the photos forever.

Geri took pictures with Hunter after I did. She kissed Hunter in the last of her pictures. That was enough to set her to crying. She began to sob uncontrollably. My eyes also filled with tears. She handed

Hunter to Samantha, and then ran out of the room. She simply said, "I am sorry. I cannot do this."

Sandy followed her to make sure she was okay. We just stood there, tears in our eyes.

❧❧❧❧❧❧

The morning of my first 30-hour call day back at Children's, Hunter's nurse paged me. He was again vomiting more than usual and the Wilsons were worried. When I arrived, Sam and Jon were both tearful. They showed me what Hunter had thrown up and it was brown in color. Jon said, "Does that mean it is blood?"

I replied, "Most likely, it is at least dried blood. I really want to do what we can to minimize his need to vomit. It seems the act of throwing up is risking a bleed of some sort."

Sam and Jon nodded in agreement. Sam said, "We were talking and we think we might want to give him as much as we can through the IV. We know it is not the same as formula, but we do not want him throwing up. And, he is not comfortable right now. So, we want him comfortable."

I agreed with their decision, so we pulled out the nasogastric tube. We used the IV he already had in place to hydrate him and keep his sugars in balance, which seemed the most important issues at the time. The formula going through the tube had been causing Hunter to vomit and bringing about more distress for his family. Hunter seemed to be more at ease the moment the tube was out of his nose, and his comfort spread to the whole Wilson family.

That night, the Wilsons appeared relieved for my first overnight shift. They said they were glad I would be there with them if anything happened. It also meant we would be able to spend more time together, and I would get more quality time with Hunter. The night proved to be as busy as always, so my time with the Wilsons was unfortunately only a few minutes here and there. Before heading home on Saturday morning, I made sure to check in and say good-bye to the family. They seemed to be holding up well, in good spirits. I reminded them I was off the next day. Jon said, "Well, it's about time. You are here everyday. We will miss you, though."

I countered, "You will not have to miss me too much. I will probably stop by in the evening to say hi. I do not want Hunter thinking I forgot about him."

Sam said, "You should bring Xavier. We have heard so much about him and we would love to meet him." Everyone else agreed. I told them I would try. I kissed Hunter. He looked up at me, a slight frown forming. I said, "Don't cry, little man. I will be back tomorrow. I love you."

Over dinner that night, I told Xavier the Wilsons wanted to meet him. He said he wanted to meet them too. He already felt he knew them. He was a little worried though. I had talked about Hunter everyday. He knew Hunter was sick and did not know what to expect. He expressed his concerns, "I have not really ever seen a baby who is sick. And, what if I do not know what to say to them?"

I said, "Well, I will tell you what I can now. His skin is quite yellow. He is also swollen, mainly in his belly. But, otherwise, he is just a beautiful baby. I hope he is awake so you can see him play. As for what to say, trust me, the Wilsons will likely do all the talking. And, be yourself. They will not expect you to know the right things to say. I do not even know the right things to say. I will be there with you, so hopefully, that will help you to feel more comfortable."

"Okay, well, I do want to meet them so let's do it," Xavier replied, still looking a bit nervous.

❧ Chapter Eight ❧

Xavier and I walked into the hospital on Sunday evening and headed to the second floor. I knocked on the door of room 2026 and found the whole family inside around Hunter's bed. I said, "Hi, everyone. This is Xavier."

They got out of their chairs, taking turns shaking Xavier's hand and giving him hugs. It was like a family reunion. Then, I said, "Xavier, I want you to meet my boyfriend, Hunter."

He replied, "Wow, Hunter, you are cute. You are the guy whose picture is on my wife's nightstand," at which the Wilsons laughed.

Hunter opened his eyes and looked up at Xavier. Hunter kept his blue eyes on Xavier the whole time he was in the room. I said, "He is checking you out."

Sam added, "Yeah, he is thinking, who is that guy with My Rose?"

Hunter was quite awake that night. He played with his toys and especially reached for the monkey, Rose. Well, he played with the tag on the monkey – always his favorite part. He seemed happy and content just spending time with us. He must have known we had come to the hospital just for him. I had told Xavier about Hunter's love of camouflage and his favorite blanket. Hunter was covered with it and playing with the tassels for most of the time we were there.

We talked with the family, and I noticed Xavier felt comfortable. I knew the Wilsons very well by that time, so I never doubted Xavier would get along with them. We shared stories about our times in the hospital with Xavier. Some I had already told him, but he sat and listened to them again. Some were new to Xavier, including one Nanny told about a day the previous week.

Nanny began, "Oh, Xavier, your wife is so funny. We had all ordered pizza and, of course, we invited Rose to join us. She was sitting on the bench by the window, watching Hunter play with his uncle, Jim. I had my eye on her the whole time. Do you know she eats her pizza backwards?"

"What do you mean?" Xavier asked.

"She eats the crust before the rest of the pizza and even then she sometimes does not eat the rest. I called her out on it and probably embarrassed her in front of everyone!"

"You did not embarrass me. You just said that you do not understand; you said it must be a *city* thing," I replied with a smile and a hug for Nanny.

Xavier laughed at the story, saying, "Well, I have been married to her for awhile and I still do not understand everything she does. So, you are not the only one."

"Gee, I can just feel the love you guys. Thanks," I said.

There was so much laughter and happiness in the room, it was sometimes tough to remember we were visiting with a sick child. I knew how lucky Hunter was to be surrounded by such love.

As it began to get late, Xavier and I said good night. I kissed Hunter. He looked at me and at Xavier one more time. Xavier said, "Bye buddy. Nice meeting you." I told the Wilsons I would see them in the morning.

That night, I felt Xavier was more a part of my work than he had ever been before. He had looked into Hunter's eyes. He had seen the smiles of the Wilsons. He knew them now. It was real for him too.

We came home and decided to watch some television. The show we chose focused on a group of people helping a family with an ill son. The boy had undergone heart transplantation and had many complications from his treatments. The special guest on the show was an inspirational singer. He came into the children's hospital where the boy was a patient and sang an original song. My eyes filled with tears as I listened to the words. It was about parents dealing with the illness of their son and asking God for the strength their son needed, along with strength for themselves. It was a beautifully poignant song, especially that night. It made me think of Jonathan and Samantha.

As I tried to fall asleep that night, I could not get the lyrics of the song out of my head. It was hard for me to imagine that multiple other families were also going through what the Wilsons were. I found it challenging to get my mind around one child dying in a hospital room. It was even more difficult to imagine the same scene playing out all over the country. Sometimes, things did not make sense, and I went off into my dreams thinking about Hunter's case.

During his first hospitalization, Hunter had improved without a clear reason why. After the vomiting incident and some rough days this time around, again Hunter seemed to turn a corner. He was awake more often, and when he was awake, he was more playful and interactive. It was hard to say what led to the change. I realized medicine did not have all the answers. As physicians, we sometimes needed to leave things in the hands of something or someone bigger than us.

The moods of the Wilson family improved as Hunter continued to push along. During those days, many of Hunter's loved ones came to visit and I had the privilege of meeting them. As they did months ago, Sam and Jon always introduced me as "Hunter's Rose." And, the same response still followed, "Oh! You are the Rose we have heard so much about."

One day, yet again, I received a page from Hunter's nurse. This time, when I returned the call, it was good news. The nurse told me the pictures from the photographer had arrived. The Wilsons requested I come to their room and see the photos. We sat around Hunter on the bed and looked through the pictures. The albums were such a wonderful tribute to our handsome, little man. They were arranged like a wedding album with the pictures in black and white to minimize the jaundiced color of his skin. The photos were gorgeous and so many of them captured Hunter in perfect, real-life moments. The ones taken of the two of us made me cry. He looked so comfortable in my arms it took my breath away.

There was one picture Sandy wanted me to see in particular. She said, "It looks like you are our angel." I asked what she meant. She responded, "You will see."

I flipped through the pictures, and then I saw it. There was a picture of the Wilson family sitting on the couch. The way the lighting caught the window caused my reflection to show up above Poppy's shoulder. It looked as though I was watching over them. Sandy said, "See, we always knew you were this family's angel. Now, we have proof."

I took one of the pictures of Hunter and me and placed it in the cover of my hospital badge. It was a special way to carry him with me wherever I went. I continued to have it with me through my years of residency. People would stop and ask who the adorable baby was. Each time, I had the opportunity to share stories of Hunter.

෨෨෨෨෬෬෬

I found Hunter occupied my thoughts quite a bit, even when I was at home. I would call my mom and dad frequently to let them know I was doing okay. I could tell from their voices they were worried about me. They had heard about Hunter throughout the months, so when I shared the devastating news about his diagnosis, they were sad as well. I knew they were proud of the bond I formed with the Wilsons and they told me so all the time. My mom had always been such an optimistic person. She would say, "Maybe something will change. Maybe he will be okay. Are you sure there is no chance?" I hated having to tell her Hunter was going to die no matter what we did, because I still did not want to believe it myself. My parents were glad when I called and Hunter was still pushing along. I knew they were concerned for the one call we were all dreading.

Even when he was not feeling well, Hunter had a way about him. All babies do, but Hunter's way was unique. He had a sense of humor. The neurologists would probably not have believed us. They would likely have said, "According to his MRI, he was likely not displaying a more mature sense of humor." Those of us who truly knew him recognized the little nooks and crannies of his amazing personality. He knew what to do to make us smile. Sometimes, he was too tired to perform. Sometimes, he would whine out of frustration that his little body could not do it. Yet, sometimes, he would overcome it all and act as only little Hunter was able.

For instance, Hunter was a bit of a "drama king." When he was sick of hearing everybody talking, and wanted some peace and quiet, he let us know. He never liked it when I came in during rounds and presented him to the team. I realized he did not like hearing about the swelling of his belly, how easily he could bleed, or his poor nutritional status. I cannot say I blamed him. I did not enjoy having to talk about those things either, but it was part of being his doctor.

When Hunter did not want to hear what was being said, he would grab the edges of his camouflage blanket and dramatically pull it over his head. We would worry he could not breathe. We would look under the blanket and make sure he was okay. He always was. He would stay under there until we stopped talking or until he had enough alone time.

My attending physicians did not believe the stories I told of Hunter interacting with us. Then, one day, right in the middle of rounds, Hunter proved them wrong, grabbed the blanket and tossed it up over his head. Even my attending laughed. He could not believe the little sense of humor. Then, when Hunter pulled the blanket back down, he looked around as if he knew exactly what he had done. He knew we thought it was the cutest thing in the world. Somehow, among his fatigue and muscle weakness, he was able to muster up the strength to be dramatic and make us smile. It was pure Hunter. Too bad the neurologists were never there to witness it.

It was troublesome to leave for home in those days. I was tired and knew I needed to be in again the next morning, but I still could not leave. I was concerned something would happen while I was far from the hospital. Everyone had my cell phone number - the family, the nurses, and the residents on call - but I was still worried. As much as I never wanted anything to happen to Hunter, I also knew that if something did, I wanted to be there. I would sit at home on my nights off, with my pager and cell phone, one in each hand. I was not willing to miss that page or call. If it had come, I would have been in my car and at the hospital as soon as possible.

The Wilsons knew how much extra time I was spending at the hospital. They knew not many doctors would stay over-shift to be with a family. They knew how special Hunter was to me, and how special they were. I recognized each time I kissed his forehead might be the last. We knew the next time we saw each other might be because I had been called in for something bad.

The worst part was no one knew how Hunter would pass away. We realized it was coming, apart from some miracle. The true fear became how it would happen. His coagulation studies – the ones that told how well his blood was clotting – were off the charts in the wrong direction. That meant if he bled from anywhere, he was going to bleed uncontrollably. Even the spots on his heels where the nurses had checked glucose levels days before would still occasionally ooze blood.

The biggest concern was he would bleed from his intestines or stomach. This could mean he would have a large amount of blood in his stool or vomit, and he would not stop bleeding. As sad and terrible as it was to think about, there had to be a plan for just that situation. If it occurred, the nurses were to wrap Hunter in blankets, hand him to Samantha, and let things happen as the family had requested. There was a pile of blankets on the table by the door for that purpose. It was a constant reminder of what could be. The hope was he would bleed into his brain and slowly pass away, simply fall asleep. The *hope*, is that not terrible? That was the *best*-case scenario. It was difficult to stomach, but it was constantly on the minds of those who loved him.

One night, as I was sitting at home worried the hospital would call, my phone buzzed. My heart jumped to my throat, but I saw it was my sister Jenica on the line. Deep breath. She called to tell me her office wanted her to go to Hong Kong for a few months. She practiced as a lawyer and her firm had affiliates all over the world. It was a huge step for her career, and I was excited for her. It was funny how I could be so busy at work with a million things going on, and I had not caught up with my family as much as I would have liked. Then, one of them would call and it was as if we had just spoken. I knew she was going to have an amazing time. She asked if Xavier and I wanted to visit while she was there. I said, "As much as we would love the opportunity, given my bank account is close to the negative and I am an intern, which means my life is not my own, I do not think it is going to happen." She laughed. We talked for a little while longer and then said "good night." Thank goodness, it was a happy phone call.

The next day, in particular, Hunter was especially playful. Whether that meant reaching up and grabbing his toys, or more often the tags on his toys, or playing with his family's name badges, those were some of the happiest times. The whole mood in the room changed whenever he was awake and playing, and that day was no different. His energy was up, and we were feeding off it. Everyone perked up and the focus was 100% on Hunter. As usual, it was my pager beeping that interrupted the fun. I always hated when it happened.

When I was a medical student, pages were more likely to be messages from friends. Now that I was an intern, pages were real, and I could not avoid them. The Wilsons would laugh with each page, wondering whether it was a question I could answer on the phone and stay with them, or whether I would have to go back to work. On Hunter's playful day, my pager had already beeped one or two times while I was in his room. On the third beep and buzz, Hunter looked me right in the eye. I think he finally had enough of it. I pulled the pager out of my pocket and Hunter reached for it. He had a way of grabbing at things with his index finger and thumb, and he tried to take hold of my pager. He was quite the perfectionist, and became frustrated when he was unable to grasp the pager in his fingers.

I said, "Oh, do you want to play with it? It might be a little heavy for your tiny hands, but I will help you."

I held the pager, letting him touch the front. It beeped again, and in perfect Hunter-form, he reached for it, pushed it away and whined, "Aaah!"

We laughed. I said, "I know, Hunter. That is how I feel about it too." He wanted me to stay and play, but I had to see another patient in the emergency room. I said goodbye to everyone and kissed Hunter on the forehead, as usual. I still think of that moment when my pager beeps at inopportune times or when I have just closed my eyes to rest. Sometimes, I just want to say, "Aaah!"

ঌ Chapter Nine ট

Later in November, I was again on-call overnight, this time from a Saturday into a Sunday. The Wilsons had memorized my call schedule. I did not realize it at the time, but looking back, I think they were more comfortable when I was on-call. If something happened, they wanted someone who knew and loved Hunter to be there. As soon as I arrived on Saturday morning, the Wilsons welcomed me and Vince said, "Guess what we are having for dinner?"

I replied, "You know you guys are spoiling me? You are way too sweet."

He said, "We are repaying you for all you do for our Hunter."

"I want to take care of Hunter. I hope you do not think I am only in this for the food. I mean, it is a perk, but it is not the only reason," I replied with a wink.

We laughed as Vince said, "Well, either way, we are having ham stew with homemade noodles for dinner."

"Mmm," I sounded, "Cannot wait."

I knew I would be busy that day, but I promised to stop by. Jon asked if I wanted to come in their room to watch the Notre Dame football game. I said, "I have to make Hunter into a fan, so I will be here as much as I possibly can."

I was able to sneak away from work during the first quarter of the football game. Hunter was awake, so I sat in bed with him, and we watched the game together. I said, "I should have bought you a Notre Dame shirt to wear. Then, you could really be a fan!"

During the broadcast of the game, I pointed out places on campus to the Wilsons. When Notre Dame made a good play, I tried not to cheer too loudly since noises bothered Hunter. I would hold his little hand and raise it in the air, saying, "Go Irish!" Hunter seemed to be enjoying it. I wanted to stay with the Wilsons for the whole game, but I still had work to do and was only able to be there for a little while. Notre Dame lost that day, but I will remember the game with fond memories, as it was the game I watched with my little Hunter.

When it was time for dinner, Natalie, Hunter's nurse, paged me saying, "Ham stew emergency in Family Lounge. Stat."

I walked into the lounge laughing. Jon asked if I liked my page. I said, "It happens to be my favorite kind of page. And, luckily, I have a break to eat."

We sat and ate together, and, as usual, the stew was fantastic. I kissed Vince on the cheek and thanked him for making my call night better. I told him I still needed to stop by and hang out with Hunter for a bit. He said he understood.

I walked down the hall to room 2026 and knocked on the door. Sam and Nanny, Hunter's great-grandmother, were in the room. I said, "Hi there. I hope you had some stew."

They said they had. As soon as I spoke, Hunter opened his eyes. He always seemed to know when I was in the room. He looked up at me with his gorgeous blue eyes, still sparkling, even with the yellow glow of jaundice.

I sat on the bed next to him, "getting my Hunter time." I loved looking at him, holding his hand, or just being next to him. In those days, he occasionally had a hard time with any kind of touch. It sometimes seemed even the weight of his blanket was too much for him. None of us really understood why, but when he did let us touch his face, or hold his hand, we took those moments and did not let them go. It was one of those times that night; he let me hold his hand. I enjoyed about five minutes before my pager beeped, which woke Hunter. I told him I was sorry, kissed his forehead, and said "good night" to Sam and Nanny. I reminded them, "I am here all night. You know you can call me."

Sam replied, "We will be here. You can come by whenever you want."

The next morning while examining Hunter, Jon said to me, "Hey, Rose, you know Gayle, the nurse? She wore camouflage scrubs the other day to show her love for Hunter. I have not seen you wearing camo."

I replied, "Oh, so now I can only show my love by wearing camo, huh? I thought I show how much I love Hunter by all the time I spend with him."

Jon stated, "I know you love him, but we want to see some camo! It may not be your style, but we would all love to see it."

That night, I went shopping and searched for something camouflage to wear. I could not believe how much there was to choose from when I was actually looking. Even now, whenever I see someone wearing camo, I think of the Wilsons and, most of all, of Hunter. I decided on a camouflage belt. It was subtle, but it did the trick. As I was waiting in line to pay for the belt, my phone rang. It was a number from the hospital. My heart sunk to my feet and my breath caught in my throat. I looked at Xavier and he could see right through me. We both held our breath as I answered. I said shakily, "Hello."

"Rose, it is Michaela. First of all, it is not, I repeat not about Hunter, okay? Take a deep breath." Michaela was one of my co-interns. She had a question about another patient who was being discharged that night. She apologized over and over. I told her it was okay; at least it was okay once my heart began beating normally again. I finished my conversation with her and bought the camouflage belt.

The next morning, I walked into Hunter's room and proudly showed off my camouflage belt. The Wilsons loved it. Jon said, "See, now we really know you love Hunter."

Sam included, "Right, as if we were ever actually doubting that, huh, handsome man?"

I said, "I hope you do not ever doubt it, Hunter. I love you more than you know."

Sam replied, "Oh, he knows. Do not worry about that."

It was also during that week when the long days started to catch up with me. I was tired. I knew it and the Wilsons did, too. "You know you can always sneak in here and take a nap if you need to?" Jon said in response to me yawning while examining Hunter.

I reminded him, "Even though you guys do not think so because I am always in here with you; I *am* quite important. I do have work to do."

Jon responded, "Sure you do, Rose. Everyone knows you would rather just be here with us."

I replied, "Well, that is true, but unfortunately, there are a lot of other things I need to do around here too." As if the hospital gods heard me, my pager began to beep and vibrate.

I was called back to Hunter's room later that day. When I walked in, Jon and Sam had fearful looks in their eyes. Hunter was sleeping, but he did open his lovely, blue eyes for a few moments when he heard me. I asked Jon and Sam what was wrong. Jon said, "He had some red in his diaper. We think he might be peeing blood."

I said, "Okay, well, his urine has been dark for a little while now, because he is peeing off the extra bilirubin from his liver not working correctly."

Sam replied, "But this is really red."

"Okay, let me take a look." I walked over to where the diapers were sitting. Gayle, Hunter's nurse, came in to show me what they had seen. We examined the diaper, and it did look as though there were spots of blood. My heart beat a little faster as I turned to talk to my friends.

"It does look like there is a little bit of blood. That could mean many things. Likely, he has some irritation in his bladder from retaining urine during this whole process. With his coagulation studies where they are, it does not surprise me that some of those areas would bleed. I think we should probably send the urine to the lab to make sure there is not an infection causing it. But, that is up to you both."

Jon said, "Let's check it. But, if it is bleeding, does that mean it won't stop?"

It was a hard question. I replied, as best as I was able, "We know his labs do not look good. It does still look like a little bit of blood. We will keep a very close eye on it. It may continue, but depending on where it is coming from, it may stop too. We will have to wait and see."

I knew that was not the answer they wanted to hear, but we really did not know more than that. Given his labs, he could have been bleeding any-where at any time. This was an external sign of things we knew were likely going on internally. It was very scary for the family, and for all of us, to see the blood right there in front of our eyes. I tried to calm their nerves, and I could only do so much. They thanked me for coming and talking to them. I promised I would let the other doctors know, and if the team thought of anything else, I would return with the information. The Wilsons were grateful as always.

Two days before Thanksgiving, Hunter began to struggle. He was not playing as much, and he was sleeping most of the day. When he did wake up, he would cry or whine, with his little "Squeaker" squeaks, but no longer the happy type. He seemed to be in pain, but it was difficult to say where the pain was. His belly was growing bigger, and he was beginning to swell in his legs and ankles again. These were all signs his liver was continuing to fail. We gave him medicine for the pain, and small doses of medicine to try to remove some of the excess fluid from his system. It was a very fine balance, and it felt that with each day we were losing a little more of the battle.

I came into room 2026 around lunchtime and Hunter was in Samantha's arms. When I entered, I could hear Hunter breathing from the doorway. Hunter's Aunt Geri said, "Do you hear him, Rose? That is how he has been breathing for the last hour or so."

I replied, "That is definitely different than usual. Let me listen to him."

I walked to the chair where Sam and Hunter were sitting. He looked so comfortable in her arms, and she looked completely at peace holding her little man. I placed my stethoscope on his back, listening to his breaths. They were a little louder than before, but he was still moving air quite well. It was when I looked at his handsome face I realized something had changed. He was pursing his lips with each breath. Around his flawless mouth was the slightest tinge of grey. We did not have him on monitors by his family's request, but I could guess that if we did, his oxygen saturation would be lower than normal. His body seemed it was working harder to pull in the oxygen he so desperately needed to be comfortable.

I sat down, keeping my eyes locked on our precious Hunter. I said, "He seems like he is working harder to breathe. You have noticed that, I think. His color does not look too good around his mouth. I will leave the decision up to you. If we put some oxygen blowing nearby, it may give him the extra boost he needs so he does not have to work so hard. It may not help, but I think it is worth a shot. I have to tell you, if the time does come when he needs more than just oxygen, the blow-by will not keep him alive. I am thinking more that it will make him comfortable right now."

The family looked to each other for answers and support. Ultimately, the decision was Samantha and Jonathan's. Sam said, "I think we should do it. It can sit next to him. It is not like a ventilator we would have to turn off; it would just make him comfortable, right Rose?"

I answered, "As I said, when the time comes, blow-by oxygen will not artificially keep Hunter alive. I do think it would help him to breathe more comfortably. And, any effort he does not have to expend is better for him."

The entire family nodded in agreement. I let them know they did not have to have the oxygen on him all the time. I said they could use it when he was in bed, but leave it off when people wanted to hold him. They liked the idea, so we set it up. When I returned to check on him an hour later, his color had improved and he was breathing more quietly and more comfortably. The Wilsons thanked me, saying how peaceful he looked. I explained it was not a long-term fix, but it did seem to be keeping him happier. I was glad to see his lips a little pinker.

After the continuously busy day, my team let me go home a few hours early. They knew I was on-call the next day and figured I deserved an early night. I had to say "goodbye" to the Wilsons first. I walked in the room and announced I was going home. Jon's response was, "Of course. See, I said you never work around here."

I said, "Ha-ha. I only wish that was true. I am so tired; I could curl up on this tile floor and go to sleep."

They laughed. Nanny said, "Don't listen to him, Rose. We all know how hard you work and we love you for it."

I said, "Thank you, Nanny. *Not* thank you, Jon."

The space next to Hunter on the bed happened to be vacant, so I jumped at the opportunity to sit with him. The oxygen was close-by, so he was breathing comfortably. I found myself just staring at him. The family was deep in a conversation about rattlesnakes. I, on the other hand, was mesmerized by the precious little boy next to me. He was sleeping most of the time, but he would occasionally open his blue eyes, as if he was checking to make sure I was still there. "I am here, buddy," I thought to myself. I am not sure how much time went by when Sam broke my deep thoughts by saying, "Hey, Rose, we know you love us, but you need to go home, relax, and have dinner with Xavier."

Vince said, "Or, you could stay here and eat chicken stir fry with us!"

I replied, "Don't tempt me, Vince. I really should head home."

I kissed Hunter, as always, and said I would be on-call the next day. Samantha said, "Yeah, we love Rose's call days, huh, handsome man?" Hunter was too far in his dreams to acknowledge the question.

I drove home after work with visions of Hunter's face. His color had improved with the oxygen, but it was hard to say what was causing him to need the extra help to breathe comfortably. I was replaying conversations I had shared with the Wilsons, realizing how much they had become like family to me. It was in the middle of those thoughts that I attempted to change lanes to my right. For some reason, the mini-van in front of me decided to slam on his brakes at exactly the same time. I clipped the back of his bumper and felt tears fill my eyes. I knew I was not physically hurt, but emotionally, I was drained.

The driver of the van came to my window and asked angrily, "Why did you do that?" I had no response for him. Well, actually, to be completely honest, I had plenty of responses for him, but none of them were very ladylike. "Because I felt like getting in a freakin' accident today." "Because my day was not shitty enough, I figured an accident would be a great idea!" "Because I needed one more financial burden in my life when the economy already sucks." Instead, I just shook my head.

We exchanged information. The experience felt like a blur. Cars drove past us and I sat there, not really listening to the man. When he had the information he wanted, I put my car in "Drive" and took off. I do not remember getting home from there. The accident was the straw that broke the camel's back, so to speak. I pulled into our driveway and realized Xavier was not home yet. I text messaged him, "Got in accident. So sorry. I'm okay."

I have been in accidents before, but I had such guilt over this one. I knew my guilt was a result of the other emotions I was fighting. We did not have the money at that time to deal with car expenses. The holidays were approaching, and we wanted to use the money we did have to buy gifts for our families. What was I supposed to tell my insurance? "Sorry about that accident. I was thinking about a dying ten-month-old boy and how much I love him, and that is why I got in the accident. So, could you find it in your hearts to pay for it?" Those kinds of things do not work in the real world.

I walked into our apartment, pet Tucker and Jake, shut the bedroom door, and dropped down on our bed. I pulled the blankets up over my head, just like Hunter would have, and completely lost it. I cried and cried. Not only about the accident. I cried for Hunter. I cried for the Wilsons. I cried that I could not give Hunter a piece of my own liver and miraculously cure him. I cried for little Valerie who had died months ago. I cried for myself. I realized how much I had been bottling up because I did not have the time to let it out.

I could hear Tucker and Jake whining from the other side of the bedroom door. I knew they were concerned about me and wanted to give me their love, but I could not bring myself to get out of bed. Xavier came home to find me still sobbing. He climbed into bed and hugged me. I kept saying how sorry I was about the accident. He said, "Do not worry about it. Things happen. I know you are crying for more than that."

My only reply was, "Oh, X, Hunter is dying and I do not want him to."

He held me until I could not cry anymore. Of course, that left me with a splitting headache. I took a couple ibuprofen pills and Xavier and I decided to have dinner. Xavier let me talk the whole time. I was rambling, but I needed to say what was on my mind. By the time I curled into bed that night, I was exhausted, to say the least. I held my phone close to me in bed, worried I would get a call about Hunter. The call did not come. I finally drifted to sleep, although I had nightmares all night long.

৯ Chapter Ten ৵

It was the day before Thanksgiving, and I knew I should be thinking of the things for which I was thankful, but the truth was, I was angry. I could not understand why Hunter had to be so sick. I knew he had seemed to fight back in the past when the odds were against him, but I also knew I had to be realistic. He had been having a rough few days. I had seen the labs and knew his chances of bleeding somewhere were very high. I wanted to be thankful for the time we had with him, but I was sad for his family at the same time. We knew months were no longer a consideration. Weeks were possible, but unlikely. We wanted to be prepared, but as it turned out, even I was not ready for the day ahead.

I was making morning rounds, stopping in to check on my patients. Most of them were doing exceptionally well that day. I was able to sneak in and out of rooms without waking the parents and children who had already been awakened multiple times in the middle of the night for vitals, medication administrations, and the other "joys" of being in the hospital. I saved Hunter's room for last. I opened the door as quietly as possible, but I always seemed to wake Jonathan, as if he knew I was coming.

Hunter was sleeping peacefully on Samantha's chest with the oxygen lying close-by. I saw Jon's eyes flutter open and motioned him to go back to sleep, but he called me over to him. He said, "Hey, don't do that anymore."

I was taken aback not knowing what I had done. "What do you mean? What did I do?"

"Yesterday, you scared me. You sat on the bed for almost fifteen minutes, just staring at Hunter. You had a look on your face that really concerned me like you knew something that none of us knew."

I remembered sitting there the prior afternoon. I pondered what had been going through my mind. I had been thinking how beautiful Hunter was. I had been wondering how such a faultless little man was fighting through so much. I replied, "You know I can stare at Hunter for hours. I don't think I meant anything more by it yesterday than I have any other day. I just love looking at him."

"Oh okay," he said. "Well, don't do that anymore. At least smile or something."

"I promise. Sorry." I smiled, trying to show him a positive sign. In retrospect, maybe he saw something in me that I did not even see in myself. Maybe I knew something in my head while looking at Hunter that day which my heart was not willing to believe. But, I was still not at all prepared for what was to come. After talking with Jon, I listened to

Hunter's heart and lungs, examined his belly, kissed his forehead, and tiptoed out of the room.

Attending rounds began that morning, much like any other. Even though I already had one cup of coffee, I felt like I had not. I am usually on top of things, but I was one step behind that morning. I could not put my finger on it, but something was not right. I was starting a 30-hour shift, so I chalked it up to that.

Around 10 a.m. that morning, the time came to round on Hunter. Only the attending physician and I usually visited Hunter, as there were always family members occupying most of the space in the room. Dr. Murphy, my attending, and I entered, finding the smiling faces of the Wilsons. They found a way to greet us with smiles, no matter what the day or the situation. We discussed how Hunter was doing, and Dr. Murphy was pleased the oxygen was making him more comfortable. She examined his belly and relayed to the family that it would continue to be a day-to-day process. They nodded their understanding. I kissed Hunter on the forehead, hugged Vince, and asked him when we were going to get to try his amazing home-baked pretzels. He promised he would make them later that day. I told him I was looking forward to it.

After visiting with the Wilsons, Dr. Murphy and I stood by the nurses' station talking. She reiterated what I already knew, "I no longer think we have weeks. I am hoping we have days."

I agreed and replied, "Yes, I think the oxygen is making him comfortable, but he is looking a little more like he is fighting. His color is not good." She nodded and frowned. We loved the family and yet we knew how this was going to turn out.

Rounds continued and ended without event. I returned to the team room and planned to eat lunch after tying up a few loose ends. I was working on the computer when my pager buzzed. The message read, "2417-911." I had never received a 911 page before. The nurse taking care of Hunter was luckily not on the 2417 extension. So, my initial thought was, "Thank God it is not Hunter. But, what else is going wrong?"

I tried to call back, but the phone was busy. Just then, my senior resident, Hannah, ran in and said, "Rose, it is Hunter. We have to go now." My heart stopped. Not now, please.

Then, my cell phone rang. That was not a good sign. I answered and it was Natalie, Hunter's nurse. She said, "I just took Hunter's vitals. His heart rate is down to the 50s and his respiratory rate is low. Please come. As soon as I told the family, they said, 'Please, get Rose. Call her now.'"

I started running. When I arrived at Hunter's door, I saw Natalie's face and tried to keep it together. She said, "I am really worried, Rose. Samantha is holding him on her chest. He does not look good."

Hannah recommended I be the one to go in the room. She said she was right on the other side of the door if I needed her, but the family had asked for me. I walked into room 2026. The whole family turned to me, all with tears in their eyes. Sam was cuddling

Hunter on her chest and looked at me with the saddest eyes I had ever seen. She tried to smile, but she broke down and cried instead. All I could think of saying was, "I am here now. Let me listen to him."

I took the stethoscope, my hands shaking. I listened to his heart and his struggling lungs. I looked at his face. His eyes were pretty much closed, but I could still see a hint of the beautiful blue. At that point, I knew. The sparkle was fading. Even at his sickest, his eyes had still shone, had still held that Hunter glow, but in that instant, I could see the glitter was barely there. My heart broke. I could hear a faint heartbeat, but my own pulse was pounding so loud in my ears, it was hard to tell the difference. I did not hear any breaths so I asked Sam, "Have you felt him breathing?" She replied, with tears in her voice, "Only occasional gasps." As if on cue, Hunter took a big gasp of air.

I knew I had to ask, and the words were the hardest I had ever had to say. I mustered up all my strength, and yet I began crying as soon as the first word was uttered. "I need to make sure that you still do not want us to do anything else at this point. Our goal is to keep him comfortable. Is that what you want?" By that time, I was sobbing. So were all the other loving people in that room.

Sam and Jon looked at each other, and said in unison, "Yes."

Sandy, Jon's mom, said, "Please stay and be here with us."

I said, "Gather around him and give him all your love. Just be here together with him."

I tried to step back to let them have their moment with Hunter. As soon as I did, Vince and Sandy grabbed my arms and pulled me back into the group. Vince said, "You are a part of this family, and you will be here with us. You love him, too." It was so true. I loved him like crazy. There was no mistaking that.

We linked arms around the bed and took turns kissing Hunter. We tried to give Sam and Jon any reassuring words we could find. Sandy said, "Well, Rose, we already knew, and now we are sure. You are going to be the best doctor. We know because Hunter is going to be your angel."

I replied, "I hoped he would be. I will do everything in my power to make him proud."

Natalie came in at one point, as did some of my co-residents. They hugged me and asked if I was okay. I tried to redirect the attention away from myself. I would be okay. I was worried about Samantha and Jonathan. I wanted to hug them and make it better, but I could not. We went through at least 20 boxes of terrible hospital tissue.

Sandy joked, "You know, everything at this hospital has been perfect, except for the tissues. They could really improve those."

Dr. Murphy entered the room, tears in her eyes as well. She took her stethoscope and asked if she could listen to Hunter. Sam moved Hunter's little body enough so that Dr. Murphy could listen. Hunter looked like he was in a deep sleep. Dr. Murphy listened diligently to his lungs and to his precious heart. She stepped back from the bed and with a waver in her voice simply said, "I am so sorry. I do not hear a heartbeat."

In the same moment, I noticed that Hunter's great-grandfather, Poppy, was looking unsteady on his feet. I asked if he needed a chair, and he nodded his head. I moved a chair towards him and helped him to sit. As soon as he did, he leaned over, placed his head in his hands, and started sobbing. It was by far one of the saddest things I had ever seen. My heart broke a little more.

Each family member again leaned in and kissed Hunter, giving words of love and wisdom. Some things I overheard were, "You are the strongest little boy I have ever met. I love you." "You are perfect." "You are surrounded by love." It was so striking, and yet so devastating at the same time. I got my turn to kiss him and tell him I loved him. It was difficult, but I also hugged Jon and Sam and told them I loved them. They simply said, "Thank you. We love you, too."

Poppy stood up from his chair and walked towards the door. I think he needed to go down the hall and have some alone time. However, along the way, he stopped and grabbed me in a big hug, crying on my shoulder. He looked me in the eyes and said, "Thank you. Thank you so much. We love you." I said, "You are welcome. I love you all, too." It was such a poignant moment, and I cried even harder.

I knew I needed to give the family some time. I told Sam and Jon I would be right down the hall and walked to join my team in our room. Everyone hugged me while I sat and cried. I called Xavier. The second he heard my voice, he knew. I said, "Hunter just died." He said he was there for me and said he loved me. I knew he was sad too.

I attempted to eat lunch. I sat there, staring at the food, not feeling very hungry. My co-residents tried to talk about other things, but I was in a daze. I could not believe *that day* had been *the day*. Hunter was really gone. I would round on patients the next morning and he would not be there, the Wilson family would not be there. What a Thanksgiving. I did not want to be at the hospital. I wanted to be with the Wilsons. I wanted time to mourn. But, I was scheduled to work overnight.

When I returned to room 2026, the Wilsons appeared grateful to have me back. Natalie said, "They were all asking where you went."

I said, "I wanted to give you some time for your family."

"Stop, Rose, you are family." Jon replied.

Samantha was still lying in the hospital bed with Hunter in her arms. She had not budged. She said, "I do not want to move. I want to be here with him."

I responded, "You do not have to move. Nobody is taking these moments from you, okay?"

"Okay," she said with tears still filling her eyes.

Jon climbed in bed next to Sam with his arms around his wife and son. He may not have realized it, but every five minutes or so, he would lean in and kiss Sam, Hunter, or both. The love that exuded from the three of them was palpable. They still made such a gorgeous family, even after Hunter had passed.

Sam said, "Rose, he looks like he is sleeping. I know he is not, but my heart wants him to wake up and breathe. I keep thinking he will."

"I know. He really looks like he does when I come in to examine him in the mornings. He still looks so handsome," I stated.

She simply said, "Handsome, handsome, naked man."

For the next few hours, I somehow managed to admit two patients while stopping by Hunter's room as often as possible. I took histories on my new patients and performed physical exams, but to this day, it is a blur. I wrote my notes and placed orders. I answered pages and checked on patients, but my heart was not in my work for the first time. My heart was in room 2026. I was concerned for how I would do after the Wilsons left the hospital. I knew I had to be there for the whole night. It was likely going to be my longest night in the hospital, and my loneliest.

I returned to check my cell phone messages. As it turned out, Xavier had driven to the hospital to give me a hug, but I had missed his calls. It made me feel better knowing he was there for me, but I was sad I had missed his visit. I called Xavier to apologize for not getting the messages when he was at the hospital. He sounded upset and I assumed it was only because of Hunter. He said, "Umm, babe, I need to tell you something." I thought, "What now?"

He continued, "My 'check engine' light went on as I was driving home. Then, the car began to overheat. It needs to be taken in to the shop."

I asked, "Well, how are you going to come and get me tomorrow since my car was in the accident?"

He said, "I do not know. I will try to figure something out, I guess. And, there is one more thing."

I said, "Of course there is, because today has not been shitty enough."

He said, "I am sorry, but the dogs went on a rampage in the apartment. It looks like a tornado hit. They ate your computer wires, books, and your camera. They even destroyed the Coach brand camera case Jenica gave you last Christmas. I do not know what came over them."

All I could think to say was, "Maybe they read my mood last night and knew something was going on today. People say dogs know that kind of stuff."

His response was, "I think most of it was Jake. He is always the one that does things like this." This was how it went in situations about the dogs. Xavier had Tucker before he met me. Tucker was a puppy when Xavier and I first started dating, but he was always just that slightest bit more Xavier's dog than mine. Jake, on the other hand, was considered more "my dog." I had picked him out the day I found out I passed part of my medical boards. As a result, I often felt Xavier blamed Jake more often than he did Tucker. And, in the mood I was in, I could not just let the comment go.

"Oh, X, everything is always Jake's fault. It could not possibly have been Tucker. You always blame Jake. They are *both* your dogs and you should love them equally."

"I do love them both. I am sorry. I know you are upset. I just got a feeling that Jake looked guilty," he replied.

"Well, we will never know. Sorry I am so upset, I am just completely overwhelmed. God, this day has been a mess. I really wish I could come home."

He said, "Can't you ask to take the night off?"

I replied, "I am an intern. That is not an option."

He apologized again and we said "goodbye." Xavier promised he would try to figure out the car situation.

I called my parents to tell them about Hunter. Just as Xavier had, when my mom answered the phone, she knew from my voice something was wrong. All I had to say was, "It is Hunter, Mom." I heard tears form in her voice, even though she had never met him. She knew how much I loved him. She gave me support and said she and my dad were there if I needed them. I thanked her and told her I needed to get back to work. I could tell she was worried I had to be at work overnight, but with as much courage as I could, I tried to reassure her I would be fine. Although the truth was, I knew I was anything but fine. We said, "I love you" and hung up.

The next chance I had to get to the Wilsons' room, they had given Hunter a bath and put him in the cutest green outfit. I could almost convince myself he was not gone when I saw him in Vince's arms.   The Wilsons continued to pass around Hunter's body. His body - it was so hard to believe. I already missed his little spirit more than anything.

After everyone had gotten a moment with him, Sam took him back in her arms.

We sat around the room, as we had so many times in the preceding weeks. We were able to share stories, but at times, we sat in silence and looked at the handsome, little man. In one of those moments, Geri pointed out, "Look at the sky, everybody. It is the most gorgeous sunset I have seen since we have been in the hospital. That kind of sunset does not happen this time of year around here."

We looked out the window and it was ideal. The sky was various colors of purple, blue, and red. The sun was making its way toward the horizon, setting on the last day of our little Hunter's wonderful, but too short, life. Geri said through her tears, "It is for you, Squeaker." This only led to another round of crying.

In order to lighten the mood, Nanny took the floor. She began, "Rose, I have to confess something. I almost killed a punk kid in the parking lot at the drug store."

I replied, "Oh Nanny, what happened?"

A smile spread across Geri's face as she said, "She is not kidding, Rose. I had to hold her back physically."

I laughed through my tears as Nanny continued, "We had to run to the drug store about an hour ago to pick up my prescription. I had my doctor call it in yesterday and of course, we thought I would have plenty of time to pick it up." Then, she paused and looked over at Hunter.

"Anyways, so, I had Geri run me today. Neither of us wanted to leave, but I figured this was not the day to start skipping my blood pressure medication."

"I agree," I said, glad she recognized the importance of taking care of herself through these tough times.

Nanny smirked as she then said, "So, Geri was pulling into the parking lot and there was a handicapped spot open. I have a handicapped card, so I told her to pull into it. Well, just as she put on her blinker, a little red sporty car swung into the parking lot and took the spot. Some hoodlum teenager jumped out of the front seat and ran in the store. I could not believe it. There was no way in heck that kid was handicapped. And, to boot, he was probably just running in to grab a pack of cigarettes. So, I told Geri to stop the car. I unbuckled my seatbelt and was about to climb out and go after him."

Geri jumped in while I laughed, "So, I locked the doors, grabbed her arm, and told her that we did not need her getting herself in trouble today. It took some talking, but she finally calmed down."

"Well, I wouldn't say that. I was still looking for him in the store. You better believe I would have had words with him," Nanny replied.

"Oh, Nanny, I am sure you would have scared him to death. I, for one, would not mess with you. Especially not today," I said as I stood up to give her a hug.

Jon and Vince were working to pack up the room, likely more to occupy their minds than anything else. We pitched in as much as we could. My pager beeped a few times, and Sam smiled with each one. She said, "We are going to miss that."

I said, "That's funny, because I would not miss it one bit!"

We exchanged cell phone numbers since it was almost time for them to leave. Sam and Jon said they were having Thanksgiving the next day at Cassandra's house. Cassandra was one of Jon's cousins who lived nearby. They made it clear that Xavier and I were invited. Vince said, "I am cooking, so you better be there." I promised we would at least stop by.

Sam included, "You can even wear your pajamas if you are tired after your call night. We will not mind."

Nurses and staff members made their way in and out of the room throughout the early evening, paying their respects and giving their love. It was amazing to see how many people Hunter and his family had touched in their time at the hospital. Eventually, most of the items had been removed from the room, and all that remained was saying "goodbye."

I was so moved by the thought that they were going to have to leave without Hunter. I could not fathom how Sam was going to be able to put Hunter in the bed for the last time and walk out of the room. The pain would be unbearable, but as always, Jon and Sam handled the moment with such grace. Sam kissed Hunter over and over again. Jon hugged both of them in his arms.

Sam placed Hunter on his camouflage blanket and allowed Natalie to help wrap him. Each family member stole one last kiss. Tears continued to flow freely. I hugged each of them, saying, "I love you." They each thanked me, and it meant just as much each time I heard it.

Then, it was time for them to leave. Samantha and Jonathan both touched Hunter one last time before walking out of the room. Natalie and I promised we would watch over him until he was taken downstairs. When the door closed behind the family, Natalie and I were left with Hunter. We continued to cry over the little man. He was so peaceful and beautiful. We both agreed we did not think we would be sitting there on that night.

Natalie called to let the people in the morgue know Hunter was ready. I know, the morgue. It sounded so awful. I wanted to take Hunter with me, to let him sleep with me in the call room. The thought of a baby in a morgue was too much for me to conceptualize, but it was the way the hospital worked. As Natalie and I were sharing memories of Hunter, I received a page, requiring me to check on a patient on another floor.

I said, "Well, Hunter-man, I guess this is my real goodbye. You are such a beautiful boy. I love you very much. I will help to make sure your family is okay. I am so sorry, handsome man. I love you. God bless you, little one. Can I get one more kiss?"

I leaned down over his body and kissed his forehead, as I had every time I left the room before. I just knew this was the last time, and I cried even harder. I kissed him one more time and told Natalie to let me know if she needed anything. She said she would finalize the paperwork and take care of him. As I walked out of the room, I turned back to take one last glimpse of our little Hunter.

When I returned to the residents' room, I was still crying. I told Hannah about Xavier's car, the dogs, and saying goodbye to the Wilsons. She said, "Rose, I already called the chief residents. I think you should go home early."

I tried to argue. I did not want to be the girl who flaked on her duties. Hannah kept saying, "Rose, don't be silly. You have had a horrible day. It would not be good for you or the patients if you stayed. Go home and help your husband and take some time to relax, okay?"

I finally caved in and agreed. She paged the back-up intern and asked her to come into the hospital. I called Xavier to tell him I needed a ride home. He did not know how he would get to the hospital. I said I would try and call Kyle, who lived the closest to us at the time. When Kyle heard about Hunter, I could hear sadness in his voice. I also told him about our car issue. He replied, "Well, I am about two hours away on my way to a friend's house for Thanksgiving, but I can turn around."

I said, "No, do not be silly. Have fun, please. We will figure it out."

I could tell he felt bad. I tried to reassure him. Just then, Xavier came through on call waiting. I switched lines and he said, "I am on my way. Your car is running fine right now. I should be able to get at least to the hospital and back."

I was so glad I was able to tell Kyle we had a plan. I clicked back over to Kyle's line and told him. He sounded less worried. "Okay," he said, "just call if you need anything." I thanked him and told him we would get together once he returned to town. I found out later he had called my parents after hanging up with me to make sure he had made the right decision. I was grateful to hear they had reassured him.

When Xavier arrived and I climbed in the passenger seat, the floodgates opened again. I tried to explain the emotional roller coaster I had been on that day, but the words would not come out initially. When we got closer to home, I found my voice. I had been thinking about something all day and I felt I could finally put my thoughts into words.

I fought through my tears and said, "So, today, something really struck me. I mean, obviously, many things struck me. But, one thing stood out. I have told you that Hunter had been made 'comfort care.' I had liked that terminology because it felt right. We were making him comfortable. But, today, when Hunter's heart rate and respiratory rate started to go down, the Wilsons said, 'Get Rose.' I ran the second I knew, of course, but I could not change anything. I was Hunter's doctor and I was not running to save him; I was running to be there with them when he died."

Xavier nodded as I continued, "I finally understood why they wanted me there. They felt more comfortable knowing I was at the bedside. I had no miracle cure. I could not make him better in that moment, but they still wanted me there. They wanted me with them because I was Hunter's doctor and that comforted them. It was then I understood 'comfort care' could mean different things, depending on how you looked at it. But, honestly, Hunter's death was as touching as it could have been. I was honored to be a part of it, and to offer the comfort I could."

"I am sure the Wilsons were glad and comforted to have you there. You were the one they asked for," Xavier said.

"I know."

We finally arrived home. We walked inside and Tucker and Jake ran to me instantly and covered me in kisses. To this day, I truly believe their bad behavior was related to a sense something was not in order. The world had lost an amazingly perfect little boy, and things were clearly a little off-balance because of it.

♥ Chapter Eleven ♥

Thanksgiving was a bittersweet day. We had already accepted an invitation to Gil's sister's house for dinner. Yet, I also wanted to spend time with the Wilsons. We decided to begin the day with the Wilsons and then move to Gil's party for dinner.

After a night of crying myself to sleep, I could not wait to see the Wilsons, knowing it would help me feel closer to Hunter. Jon answered the door when I rang the bell. He immediately hugged me and we both had tears in our eyes. The sadness in the house was overwhelming, but as always with the Wilsons, so was the love. Cassandra and her daughter, Kristen, had a little dog named Midnight, who was a black peanut of a dog. I could only think Tucker and Jake had both made poop bigger than Midnight, but, of course, I did not say that.

Xavier and I were welcomed with open arms. I sat down next to Nanny and Poppy on the couch, both of whom pulled me closer to share hugs. It felt like being with family. I told them I had been sent home early the night before. Sam said, "Oh, thank goodness. We were sitting here worried about you being at the hospital after the day we all had." Yet again, they worried about me on the worst day of their lives. I had called the Wilsons selfless before, but they continued to amaze me.

We sat on the couch, talking and reminiscing about Hunter. Xavier found a new friend in little Midnight while I had the pleasure of looking through Hunter's baby book. Sam and the whole family had contributed to it the night before. There were lots of pictures and Hunter's birth announcement. It made me cry, but I loved seeing it. One page listed "My Favorite People." The line read, "My mom and dad, My Rose." I thought to myself, "You were one of my favorites too, Hunter-man." The part of the book that took my breath away was the end. There were pages for 11-months and one-year-old. Those were pages that would never get the chance to be filled. It was not fair and everyone in the room knew it.

As we sat talking, I was overwhelmed with the delicious smells from the kitchen. I said, "Vince, it smells fabulous. I already miss your cooking. You realize we never had those homemade pretzels."

He said, "Other people wanted to cook today, but I kicked them out. And, I promise to make you the pretzels some day."

"I will hold you to that," I said. "By the way, I want to let you all know, we are going to need to head out early to get to our friend's house. We do not want to intrude on your dinner."

Nanny said, "You are not intruding. Do not say that. You can sit with us until you have to go."

Vince included, "And you better have at least a few bites or you will break my heart."

"Okay, if I must," I replied with a wink.

A bit later, Cassandra walked into the family room and said, "Well, dinner is about ready, so I was hoping we could all say a prayer."

We stood and joined hands. Cassandra led the blessing. She said, "This Thanksgiving, I think we are saddened by the events of the last few days, but we are also thankful for the gift of Hunter. We wish he was here with us, but we know he is looking down. We are thankful to be together, to have a room full of people who loved Hunter. Thanksgiving will always be a time when we will miss Hunter more, but I hope it will also be a time to remember how blessed we were to have known him. We love you, Hunter. May God watch over you and help us through these hard times. Amen."

The family moved to the kitchen, wiping tears from their eyes. Vince snuck me into line, telling me to take some food. Sam pulled a bench up to the table so Xavier and I could join the family. As if I expected any different, the food was delicious. It tasted so much like my family's Thanksgiving dinner and again I felt at home.

When it was time for Xavier and me to leave, I knew it was going to be hard to say goodbye. I stood up and said, "I am sorry to interrupt the end of dinner, but we are going to have to head out. I wanted to say thank you for dinner and for every-thing. Thank you so much for giving me the privi-lege of being Hunter's doctor and for inviting us into your family. I am so lucky to have known all of you. Please know I love you and I will miss you each dearly."

Each family member in turn stood up from the table and gave me kisses and hugs. With each "goodbye," my eyes filled more with tears. It proved to be very difficult to say "goodbye" to people I had come to know and love. Poppy held me a little tighter and said, as he had at the hospital the day before, "Thank you, Rose. Thank you."

When I hugged Jon and Sam, we cried. They continued standing at the top of the stairs waving as we left. They had become such good friends, and I knew we would not be seeing each other as often as we would have liked. We promised to keep in touch, and I actually believed we would. I told them to call me with anything they needed.

Throughout the next days, Sam, Jon, and I text messaged frequently. Whether it was to say we were having a "missing Hunter" moment or to say "Hi" or "I miss you" or "I love you," the texts came often. I found myself writing to the two of them more than I had to some of my other friends. I wanted so much to be a source of strength for them during that time.

An email arrived at one point from Samantha. She wanted to tell me that a company had written a song about Hunter. She attached a copy of the audio version to the email. She included in her message, "I am warning you. It might make you cry." I clicked on the link and listened, while tears filled my eyes once again.

The song was simply titled "Hunter Lee Wilson." The lyrics included lines about all of Hunter's favorite things. It talked about his giggles and his smiles, all the things I missed the most. I must have listened to it five times in a row. Each time, my heart caught when I heard the line, "Dr. Rose Gorman is the best." I could not believe they had included me in something so beautiful. The song would always be a part of their family, and I knew I was forever linked to them as well. I was so blessed to have met this family and to have cared for Hunter.

The song reminded me of something remarkable. I was Hunter's *doctor*. I realized what an honor that truly was. Every patient I treated was in my care and at any given moment, I was his or her doctor. That was a huge role to fill. I realized if I had no other success in my intern year, I had succeeded in being Hunter's doctor. I did not save him. He passed away while under my care, yet I still succeeded.

My communication with the Wilsons continued uninterrupted, including while I was at work. I was having a hard time being back at the hospital, walking past room 2026 in particular. When I needed to share my feelings with someone, Jon and Sam were only a text message or an email away. Plus, I was lucky to have Xavier to listen to me as well.

Given my busy schedule, it was rare that I would take the dogs for a walk by myself. There were times I would join Xavier, but often, it was difficult to pull me off of the couch. One morning, however,

Xavier had to work and I had the day off. So, I walked the dogs. It was a crisp, cool morning, which was refreshing to my tired body.

At one point along the walkway, I let Tucker and Jake off of their leashes to run around and do their business. I watched as Tucker circled around, sniffing at everything in his path. He began to squat, which signaled me to bring the plastic bag. When I bent down to pick up the droppings, I noticed something shiny in the pile. I was taken aback, until I made out the engraved word "Coach" on the shiny piece of metal. It was the zipper from my Coach camera bag that had been eaten in the dog rampage the day Hunter passed away. Immediately, I thought with a smile, "Sure, it was all Jake's fault. I knew Tucker was involved."

All in good humor, as I truly love both dogs and I had forgiven Xavier for blaming Jake, I pulled out my phone to text Xavier. I wrote, "Busted. Tucker just pooped out the Coach camera bag zipper. I would save it for you to prove it, but you probably believe me!"

He texted back, "Ha-ha. Guess you found your proof."

≪≪≪≪≪≪≪

A week after Thanksgiving, Jon text messaged to say everybody was going to wear something camouflage on the day of the funeral. The service was going to be held in Samantha's hometown, which was hours away, so I was not able to make it. However, had it not been for having to work at the hospital, come hell or high water, I would have been there. Since I could not be there in person, I knew I had to be there in spirit by wearing camo for Hunter. I took Xavier shopping the night before the funeral. I found myself a camouflage shirt and Xavier decided he would wear my camo belt.

I woke up the morning of the funeral missing Hunter and the Wilsons more than ever. I hated that I had to be at work, but I knew everyone understood. I put on my camouflage shirt and sent both Sam and Jon a text message. I wrote, "Xavier and I are both wearing camo for Hunter. My love and prayers are with you all more than ever today."

I received a text message back from Jon shortly after. He wrote, "Thank you. We are heading to the service now. Everything is going well. We are holding up okay. Wish you could be here."

I wrote, "I want nothing more than to be there. I would rather be there with you than here at work. Tell everyone I am thinking of them and I love them."

He texted back, saying, "We love you too. Thank you for everything." I continued to receive messages from both Sam and Jon throughout the day to let me know everyone was hanging in there as much as could be expected. In a way, it was harder being away from everyone and being emotional by myself at work.

The day after the funeral, Sam emailed asking me to listen to a song that reminded her of Hunter. It was a country song about children dying too young. I had heard the song before, but not since Hunter had died. I downloaded it onto my computer and pressed play, tissues in hand.

The song only confirmed why I had always loved country music. The lyrics had a way of saying exactly what I was feeling, and this song was no different. Sitting there listening to the song, thinking of Hunter, I was also reminded of a time with my former students when a country song touched my heart. I loved moments when a song could take you back in time to special memories. I think it was what made certain songs so poignant.

I remember arriving at the school where I was teaching seventh grade on September 11, 2001. I had been listening to a CD in my car, oblivious to what was going on in the world around me. I walked into the office, as I did any other day. I overheard one of the secretaries saying, "It is going to be one of those days, I guess."

I was about to leave the office and head to my classroom when the secretary said, "Rose, the phone is for you. It is your mother." The room went silent. I could not understand why everyone looked so concerned. I said, "What? She probably has a question to ask me and she could not get through on my cell for some reason."

I felt eyes on the back of my head as I walked to the other room to pick up the call. I said, "Hi Mom. What's up?"

She said, "I wanted to let you know that Dad is okay."

I replied, "Gee, thanks for sharing. Should I have been worried?"

She said, "Well, he is in New York. I did not want you to worry."

I responded, "Am I missing something?"

"Oh, Rose, do you not know what happened?"

"Obviously not." My mom then went on to describe the events at the World Trade Center. I was blown away, and of course, everything finally made sense. I realized why everyone looked so worried and why my mother calling was such a big deal. I thanked her and told her I loved her, asking her to pass along the same to my dad.

I walked to my classroom, not knowing what to expect. I turned on our television and watched the news. I caught up quickly in the few minutes I had before my class arrived. When they finally walked in, I could tell some of the kids were very upset. We had a talk during first period about all that had tran-spired. Then, there was a prayer service for those who died. We tried to keep the day as normal as possible for the students, but there were moments we had to step back and talk or reflect on the events of the day.

A few weeks later, my class and I were on our way to a field trip. I was riding in a car with two of my students, Rose and Abby. Rose and I had bonded immediately because we shared the same name. Abby was her best friend and they had both come to help me set up my classroom before the first week of school. Rose said, "Miss Young (my maiden name), have you heard the new country song about teachers?"

I said I had not. She said, "We want to play it because it reminds us of you, especially because we shared September 11th with you."

She put in the CD and started the song. My eyes filled with tears at the third verse and refrain,

" *For my parents, she spoke of JFK,*
a president taken in his prime.
For me, she spoke of a space shuttle,
when it crashed, it seemed to stop time.
For my child, she spoke of the towers,
two planes from the sky,
the lives taken that day will always be a crime.
School remained our sanctuary
even as the world went crazy.
She reassured us that things would be okay.
She stood at the front of the class
with her eyes full of tears.
She spoke of what had happened
and helped to calm our fears.

She was not my mom, she was not my dad.
She was not the best friend that I ever had.
But she held my hand and she wiped my tears.
Thank God, she was my teacher;
And, I will remember her all my years."

Abby said, "See, it is like you."

Rose and Abby brought me a copy of the CD a few days later. I still play the song on each anniversary of September 11th, and occasionally when I need a good cry or feel like reminiscing about my days as a teacher. I think the experience bonded us forever and the song would always be a reminder, as the country song sent to me by Samantha would make me think of our Hunter-man. I found myself listening to it whenever I needed a "Hunter moment," and that occurred quite frequently in those days.

I received a copy of Hunter's memorial card in the mail a few weeks after the email from Samantha. The memorial card included an adorable picture of Hunter, as if there was ever one that was not perfect. It also contained a poem. The words fit the situation precisely. It made me cry the first time I read it, and frankly, it is not any easier to read, even now.

> *"A heart of gold stopped beating,*
> *two shining eyes at rest.*
> *God broke our hearts to prove,*
> *He only takes the best.*
> *God knows you had to leave us,*
> *but you did not go alone-*
> *for part of us went with you,*
> *the day He took you home.*
> *To some you are forgotten,*
> *to others just part of the past,*
> *but to those of us who loved and lost you,*
> *the memory will always last."*

꙳ Chapter Twelve ꙳

Early in the new year, I found myself diving deeper into my work at the hospital to overcome the depressed feelings I was carrying with me. Being away from the Wilsons, I could sometimes imagine Hunter was still alive. Then, at random times during the day, his death would come back to me and my eyes would fill with tears. I cared for many babies during my Pediatrics residency, but I never forgot Hunter.

Sam, Jon, and I stayed in close communication during the upcoming year. They remained supportive of my career and of me. When I was having a bad day or needed someone to listen, they were often the ones to whom I turned. In the same way, I would often hear from them when they were hurting the most or when they needed to share a memory of Hunter. Our friendship only strengthened.

In January, Xavier and I made a trip to visit the Wilsons to attend a dinner and auction event benefitting the foundation that had helped them financially when Hunter was in the hospital. We wanted to support the foundation, and it meant we could see the Wilsons. We decided to share a hotel room so we could spend as much time together as possible.

When we arrived at our hotel, Xavier and I gave Jon and Sam a gift. We had an ornament made at Disney World. It was Mickey ears with "Our Angel Hunter" written on the side. When Sam and Jon opened it, I could tell they loved it immediately. Sam said, "Thank you. Hunter would love it. You know how much he loved Mickey."

I said, "I know. That is why we got it. And we tried to make it in camouflage colors."

"Thank you, Rose. Thank you, Xavier," Jon said.

We had a wonderful time at the party and the auction. We wore Hunter t-shirts in his memory, complete with some of the cutest pictures of our little man. And, of course, my outfit included my camouflage belt. I was not the only one wearing camo either, as many of the items being auctioned involved hunting, fishing, or some other outdoor activity. Xavier and I bid on a few things – well, we bid on the cup-by-cup coffee dispenser. The Wilsons loved it, and continued to laugh at what "city-folk" we were.

Xavier and Jon acted like long-lost friends, finding more in common than either would have expected. Sam and I talked the whole night long. As it turned out, other members of Hunter's family, including Aunt Geri, also came to the auction, so I was able to catch up with them as well.

Jon and I took turns buying each other beer, since the proceeds were going to a good cause. By mid-way through the evening, I was feeling a little on the tipsy side. It was then that Jon's aunt Maureen walked up to us. She said, "They want to announce us as a family during the auction. They asked if someone would say a few words about Hunter. We all nominated Rose."

"You did what?" I asked, suddenly regretting the beers. "I really hope you are kidding."

"Of course not," Maureen said with a smile. "We are all counting on you. We know you will not let us down."

I was petrified. How was I going to stand up in front of a room full of people and talk about Hunter without crying or making a fool of myself given the number of beers I had under my "camouflage belt?"

"Sam, umm, you know I love Hunter. I would do anything for him, but I am so scared to do this," I said.

I must have looked pale or nauseous, because Maureen let down her guard. She quickly inter-jected, "I am kidding, Rose. Jon put me up to it. They are going to talk about Hunter. We just wanted you to feel more like one of the family by pulling a prank on you. Sorry I scared you!"

I let out a huge sigh with a laugh as I lifted my beer to Jon's and said, "Cheers, that was a really good one. I almost collapsed from fear."

"Sorry, Rose. We would not have wanted that. We love you. Hope you forgive us," Jon replied.

"Of course I do. There is nothing about this family I do not love," I said as I hugged Maureen and Jon.

After more fun at the event, we stayed up late in our room looking through pictures of Hunter and telling stories. Sam had made copies of photos for me to choose from to make an album of Hunter. It was so much fun to see the pictures of Hunter, but as always, his eyes and his smile also made me cry.

The next day, Xavier and I had to head back home as I was scheduled to work at the hospital that night. We went to breakfast with Jon and Sam and then got back on the road. The whirlwind trip was more than worth it. We had quality time with the Wilsons and had the opportunity to support a foundation that had helped Hunter.

We all ended up seeing each other in March as well when Jon and Sam made a trip to the city. They had received word that Hunter's name would be engraved on the Memorial Wall at Children's Hospital. Jon and Sam stayed with Xavier and me that weekend and we all visited the hospital to see the wall. I knew it would be hard for the two of them to return to the hospital. The last time they had been there was the day Hunter had passed away. We visited the wall, and it was moving to see the name Hunter Lee Wilson. I was able to find some nurses and staff members who had worked with Hunter, and they visited with Jon and Sam.

We enjoyed our weekend together, still talking quite a bit about Hunter. Jon and Sam were able to meet my brother, Kyle, and they acted as though they already knew each other. It was moving how sad experiences really brought people together. On the day the Wilsons headed home, we made the hour drive to a famous hunting store close to our home. It was quite an experience for Xavier and me. There was more camouflage in that store than I had seen in my whole life. I could tell why the Wilsons loved it there. I was slightly taken aback by the stuffed animal heads mounted on the walls, but I did manage to find a pair of camouflage pajama pants to buy. It was an experience to remember, one I would not have had with any of my friends other than the Wilsons. After that wonderful weekend, I found myself looking forward to any opportunity I had to see Jon and Sam, and Xavier did too.

The end of intern year and the beginning of my second year of residency kept me very busy. In clinic, I kept a picture of Hunter on my desk. It was hard to pick a favorite photo, but I chose the one of him in the purple outfit they had taken especially for me. The smile on his face and the sparkle in his eyes kept me going when I felt overwhelmed. On the day he passed away, Sandy had said he would be my angel during my career. Having his picture there on my desk reminded me of his presence. And, I never took the picture of Hunter and me out of my badge either.

August 8th of that year proved to be a big day in our family. We knew it was coming, but I do not know that we were truly prepared, least of all Jenica and Tim. August 8th was the day the triplets were born. I remember receiving the call in the middle of the night. At first when my phone rang, I jumped out of bed, thinking I was on call at the hospital and had missed my pager. When I heard Kyle's voice on the other end, I registered what was happening. I woke Xavier and we headed to the hospital.

Given I was a doctor, Jenica asked I be present up until she went into the operating room for her caesarian section. Tim kept trying to convince her to let me be the one to actually go in the operating room, but she reminded him, "You are the one who did this to me, so you will be the one in there with me." The petrified look in Tim's eyes told me he still wanted it to be me, yet he relented. That was love.

The triplets arrived without complication, although they did have to be monitored in the neo-natal intensive care unit, or NICU. Jenica was the proudest of mothers. To think three weeks prior she had been in court at trial, and now here she was giving birth to three babies. As if I had not admired her already, I sure did in that moment. She was amazing. I was wondering whether Xavier and I could handle one child during my residency, and here she was with three as a practicing lawyer.

My family made a trip to the NICU to visit the babies. It was hard to say which one was the cutest, and it would probably have been unfair to vote. Brody had a smirk on his face from the moment he was born. I knew he was going to be a trouble-maker, but he was going to need to be able to hold his own with two sisters. Brooke had the rosiest cheeks I had ever seen on a newborn. She glowed and I wondered if she would need to wear blush when she grew up. Bridget was the smallest of the three and had a flawless bow-shaped mouth. So, as I said, they were each adorable in their own way.

However, they also knew how to cry at the same time, which made us wonder how Jenica and Tim would survive.

The triplets occupied most of my free time during the next few months, after they returned home from their stay in the NICU. I was not going to let residency interfere with getting to know my nieces and nephew. Xavier and I occasionally kicked Tim and Jenica out of the house to go on a date and have some fun away from the babies. The first time we did it, we almost changed our minds. One baby was difficult; three babies took a superhero. We kept telling ourselves, "If we can handle this, we can handle one of our own someday."

In early December, I received a call from Samantha. She opened with, "Hunter's birthday is coming up. Last year, everything was still a little too fresh. But, this year, we want to celebrate and go on a trip. We are thinking Disneyland. Will you and Xavier be able to join us?"

"Hmm, December 29th. Yes, I think I have it off. We would only be able to come down for the day, though."

"That works for us. It would not be the same without you there," Sam replied.

The day in Disneyland was more fun than we could have imagined. Samantha, Jonathan, Aunt Geri, Jonathan's brother Jim, Xavier and I made the trip. The weather was beautiful for December, and we were eating up the sun, since it was snowing at home. Things seemed to go our way all day. We wondered if Hunter was looking out for us, actually we were sure he was. We rode a good number of rides and I was happy to see Sam and Jon smiling. The two of them took a picture with Mickey Mouse and asked Mickey to hold a photo of Hunter. It turned out to be the ideal souvenir.

Samantha had previously mentioned wanting to do something each year as a memorial to Hunter. They decided to purchase a brick in the walkway between Disneyland and California Adventure. Years ago, Xavier had bought me one engraved with our names and wedding date. Hunter's brick read, "Hunter Lee Wilson. Our handsome man." We each pitched in money for the brick and decided we would keep a fund each upcoming year to buy something in Hunter's memory every December 29th. I returned to work after the trip with a renewed sense of love for my job, and I had the Wilsons to thank.

❧ Chapter Thirteen ❧

In the spring of the following year, I found out I was pregnant for the first time. Xavier and I had been trying, but we never thought it would happen so fast. We were thrilled, of course, but we knew we needed to prepare our lives for a baby. After telling our families, I could not wait to call and share the news with Samantha and Jonathan.

"Hello?" Sam answered.

"Sam, it's Rose. I have some great news."

"Wonderful! I have some news to share as well," she countered, "but you go first."

"I am pregnant!" I said. "Only a month or so, but it is official."

"Oh, Rose, congratulations. I cannot wait to tell Jon. He will be thrilled as well. I was not pregnant that long ago, so please, turn to me with any questions you have. I know you may think this will be hard for me, but I could not be happier for you. Plus, since we are family, the little one will be my niece or nephew, right?"

"Of course. We would not have it any other way. So, what is your good news?" I asked.

"Well, maybe not quite that exciting, but we are moving closer to you, likely within 15 or 20 minutes. Jon got a new job within his company. So, he needs to be closer to the big city. We will almost be neighbors!"

"Sam, that is wonderful news. Plus, you will really be able to be a big part of the baby's life."

"Yep, and we have also started the paperwork for adoption. I was hoping we could have Jenica's contact information at work since you mentioned she might be able to help with all of it," Sam said, sounding excited. Given the likely genetic nature of Hunter's condition, I knew Sam and Jon had decided to adopt a child, but I had not yet heard they had started the process. It did not mean they would never consider having another child in the future, but they had their hearts set on adoption at that time. They knew there were many children in need of loving parents. I was so happy for them and believed there was a child out there who would be more than lucky to have them.

I replied, "I will email you Jenica's information. She had mentioned it last time we were all together. She would love to help. Sam, I am so glad we talked. It feels like there is so much good coming in our future, and we will be closer together to share it!"

"Exactly. I will call you when I know our moving date. But, until then, call me after your first doctor's appointment. I want to know everything is okay."

"I will, Sam. Talk to you soon. Hugs to Jon."

"Hugs to Xavier, too. Love you, Rose."

"Love you, Sam. Bye."

Time flew by, and I was completely fat with pregnancy before I knew what had hit me. It was the first time I gained weight and did not hate myself for it. The baby shower was thrown at my dad's country club. The men played a round of golf while the women had a party. Kyle called my mom the day before the shower and asked if his new girlfriend could come to the shower. According to my mom, he seemed very serious about this girl and wanted her to be involved with the family. It was the first time Kyle had requested anything like that, so my mother jumped at the chance. I believe her quote was, "Even if I don't get to eat, she can have my food. If Kyle likes this girl, I want to meet her more than anything!"

It turned out to be a pleasant day, so golf proved to be just the thing for the men. The shower was also picture perfect, primarily due to my mother's attention to detail. I was thoroughly impressed with the gifts the women brought. Each one was so unique and fit Xavier and me to a tee. We had recently learned I was carrying a girl, so the color pink abounded. This little girl was going to be very spoiled. Prilla, Kyle's girlfriend, was yet another wonderful part of the day. I could tell immediately she was a match for Kyle. She was spunky, yet respectful, and naturally beautiful with blond curly hair I would have died for.

Samantha and Jonathan had since moved to our area and were able to attend the party, which meant so much to me. Although Jon would have preferred the shooting range to golf, he told me later that he had a wonderful time. Sam had found a pink monkey stuffed animal for the baby that was almost identical to Hunter's "Rose the monkey" except it was pink. When I opened it, I knew immediately. "Oh, Sam, I love it. Thank you." When I squeezed its foot and the monkey sound erupted, I knew both Sam and I were picturing Hunter's giggle.

Not long after the shower, on September 22nd to be exact, our family expanded to include our precious Sabrina Katherine Gorman. She was a joy from the moment she was born. My parents and Xavier were at my bedside in the hospital. Jenica, Tim, Kyle, and Prilla were not far behind. Xavier's brother, Jack, also arrived, very excited to meet his new niece. He must have been thrilled, because he made it to the hospital in record time, which for him was really saying something. It was nice for the baby to be surrounded by so much love.

Samantha and Jonathan also visited within hours of the delivery. I loved having them there, but I also knew the look in Sam's eyes. She got it when she was thinking about Hunter. I knew this took her back to when Hunter was born, to all the dreams they had for him before he got sick. I said, "Sam and Jon, I wish Hunter was here to meet her. I know she would love to have him around to protect her. But, I also know Sabrina will love the child you end up adopting. They will be like cousins."

"Thanks, Rose. It is Sabrina's day and we are thrilled to be here. She is perfect," Samantha said.

"She is, isn't she?" Xavier said. "I wonder if she will have her mother's brown eyes or my blue eyes."

"It is hard to tell when they are this young, but from what I have seen, they look pretty dark, so I would have to guess she will be my brown-eyed girl," I said.

"Well, either way, she is going to be perfect," my mother stated, with all the love and pride of a grandmother. My dad nodded his head in agreement. The day continued on full of congratulations and love – an ideal way for any baby to enter the world. And, then, Melony, Xavier's sister, arrived.

Do not get me wrong; I wanted her there. She brought Xavier's parents and they proved to be as proud as my parents were. My father-in-law's eyes were full of tears when Xavier placed Sabrina in his arms. His tears always had a way of making me cry. It was the Gormans' first grandchild, so I knew it meant a lot to them. Mom Gorman said, "I know I have wanted a grandchild for a long time now, but it was worth the wait. She is all I could have asked for and more."

As for Melony, she arrived in quite a huff. She seemed upset about something, so I took the bait and asked her what was wrong. She said, "Well, Dad would not valet the car. So, we had to walk in the cold. Then, a car drove by and splashed me in a puddle. I threw up my hands expecting an apology, but he just drove by. Unbelievable. If you splash a beautiful woman with water, you really should apologize."

"Yes, I agree," I said, wondering if she had even realized I had just given birth.

She continued, "Then, my dad started laughing at me. So, I do not know how he plans to get a ride home, because he is not coming with me. Oh, I almost forgot, congratulations, you two. I am going to have to take a walk to the cafeteria to cool off. Maybe I will meet some hot doctor who will sweep me off my feet. That is why I dressed in this outfit. Don't worry, Rose, I am sure you will get your figure back soon, and then you will be able to wear these outfits too. Anyways, I am walking to the cafeteria." And, just like that, she was gone. She did not even acknowledge Sabrina's presence.

Once the door shut behind her, we all started to laugh. "Good old Melony," Xavier said.

"God help the doctors," my dad included with a smirk and we laughed again.

The first few months of Sabrina's life were harder than even I could have imagined, but I would not have traded them for the world. I turned to Jenica and Samantha for words of advice. Jenica's most frequent response was, "Call me back when you have three of them," which would always remind me to be grateful for my single bundle of joy.

I had taken maternity leave from residency, and began getting anxious about going back. We already had Mia, the triplets' nanny, set up for the days when Xavier or either set of grandparents could not watch her. Xavier loved every minute of being a daddy, and Tucker and Jake proved to be wonderful "big brothers." I had always heard Labrador and Golden Retrievers were the best dogs to have around kids, and I could not argue. They protected

Sabrina at all times and their ears perked up whenever she cried. They did occasionally wet her with
kisses, but some of her first giggle fits were related
to Tucker and Jake's antics.

Sabrina's first Christmas was filled with love.
Both my family and Xavier's family were with us at
our house on Christmas Eve. The triplets were in
heaven playing with Sabrina. It was so much fun to
watch Sabrina's eyes glow whenever any one of the
triplets paid attention to her. The gifts were abun-
dant, and we somehow made it to Midnight Mass,
even with the four little ones. Of course, by Com-
munion, all four were fast asleep, and Xavier, Tim,
Jenica, and my dad each had a baby in tow as they
walked up the aisle. I hoped they were dreaming of
Santa Claus and the happiness Christmas brought
with it.

What would be Hunter's third birthday was
right around the corner, which meant an honorary
vacation. We had been planning a trip to Victoria,
British Columbia that year. We were originally
planning to leave Sabrina with Kyle or Melony, but
then decided to bring her along. We wanted her to
know about Hunter, and figured we should start
early. This year, the travelers were Samantha and
Jonathan, Xavier, Sabrina, and I, my mom and dad,
Aunt Geri, and Jonathan's parents, Sandy and Vince.
They had flown in from Pennsylvania for the occasion.

The few days in Victoria proved to be perfect for
all of us. The first afternoon, I was sitting on the bed
with Xavier looking through a magazine detailing

points of interest in Victoria. My phone buzzed with a text message. I laughed out loud when I read, "Homemade pretzel emergency in room 211, STAT!"

Vince had surprised me by cooking the famous homemade pretzels he had promised the day Hunter passed away. They were delicious, of course, and I thought they were more than worth the wait. The surprise was a perfect tribute to the times we had all shared over meals at Children's Hospital.

Since we had bought the memorial brick the year before, we wanted to do something that year in Hunter's memory. On December 29th, Hunter's birthday, we were visiting the Royal British Columbia museum. We were wearing our Hunter t-shirts, although mine was a bit snugger after the baby weight. I found myself regretting picking the small size instead of the medium. I should have planned ahead. It turned out there was an opportunity to donate to the Children's Program at the museum to help fund field trips for students around the province. We were able to fund one school's trip in Hunter's name. We wrote a few lines about Hunter and why we had decided to donate. The words would be read to the students on the day of the field trip. It seemed like just the thing to honor Hunter that year.

After a memorable Christmas and a relaxing vacation, I returned to a challenging rotation at the hospital. Children's Hospital was busy in general at that time of year, though, so I was not surprised. It seemed parents did not want their children to be sick at Christmas, so they sometimes waited longer to bring them to the doctor. In effect, that meant sicker patients than usual in the hospital. I missed Sabrina everyday I was at work, but I had also missed my patients while on leave. My hours were long, but I was still able to have plenty of quality time with Sabrina and Xavier.

❦❦❦❦❦❦❦

The next year was a busy one, focused on working and watching Sabrina grow. Our family was as close as ever, and Prilla, Kyle's girlfriend, was fitting in with us more everyday. It was hard to believe when Hunter's fourth birthday came around in the blink of an eye.

So far, Disneyland and Victoria had been big hits. That year, we decided to take an Alaskan cruise. It was something we had all wanted to do, but none of us had ever done. Samantha and Jonathan were again the ringleaders for the trip. Jon's Uncle Ron and Aunt Maureen, along with their two daughters, Ronna and Nina, made the trip even with their busy schedules. My mom and dad came again, as did Kyle and Prilla. My mom said, "Dad has vacation saved up from years ago, so we might as well enjoy it!" Jon's friends, Matt and Colleen, from work, along with their son, Kevin, who had been Hunter's "best friend," also joined us. We were all able to relax, take in the breathtaking scenery, and just enjoy each other's company.

It was harder to plan for the yearly Hunter memorial that year, but an idea fell in our laps. While on one of our excursions in Alaska off the cruise ship, we visited an area known for its totem poles. In Alaska, totem poles were sacred, often representing people who had passed away. The place we visited was unique in that visitors were able to purchase portions of totem poles that would be carved and erected, standing forever in memory of whomever a guest wished. We used the fund saved throughout the year to purchase a portion for Hunter. His name would be engraved on a plaque next to the totem pole. The remainder of the trip was as memorable as the moment we bought the totem pole. We promised to visit the completed totem pole some time on a future trip.

After returning from Alaska, Samantha and Jonathan were busy traveling for Jon's work. They kept me abreast of what was happening with the adoption process. It proved to be a lot more difficult than they had imagined. Luckily, Jenica was their advocate and made some elements of the legal process more bearable. They hoped it was only a matter of time before they received word of a potential adoption, but weeks passed and the call never came. Their spirits were down, but given what they had already been through, they were not the type of couple to give up easily. In fact, they only fought harder.

❧ Chapter Fourteen ❧

Do you ever have one of those days when you wish you could climb back in bed? Well, February 17th of the following year was one of those days. I always slept on the same side of the bed, and therefore, always climbed out of it on the same side. So, the whole "getting up on the wrong side of the bed" did not really apply. Needless to say, it was a rough morning. As a real estate broker, Xavier had an early meeting with some of his important clients. That meant the dogs had to be fed and walked, Sabrina needed to be dressed and taken to the nanny's house, and both Xavier and I had to be presentable by 8 a.m.; easier said than done.

To start the morning, our alarm did not go off. By the time either of us realized, it was already 6:30 a.m. Seeing as we live 20 minutes from my clinic, that meant I had exactly one hour to get myself and a little 16-month-old ready and in the car. I gave Xavier the job of taking care of the dogs. From what I could hear, Sabrina was still asleep, so I decided to get myself ready first. As soon as the shampoo was in my hair, Xavier yelled into the bathroom, "Sabrina is crying and I already have the dogs on their leashes. You should get her."

"But, I have shampoo in my hair. Can you grab her a cup of milk to keep her happy for a few minutes?"

"Sure, why not? That way I can be late."

"Please, X, quickly. I owe you one."

"You owe me more than that seeing as I am also the one walking the dogs," he retorted.

I proceeded to shampoo and condition as fast as possible, shave with only one little nick, and rinse off in a little under three minutes. I threw on clothes that came close to looking presentable and ran to Sabrina's room with a towel wrapped around my hair.

Even with the cup of milk, Brina still had tears on her cheeks when I walked in the room. "I'm sorry I took so long, baby. It is going to be one of those days, okay?"

I picked her up out of the crib and placed her on the floor. Of course, she cried even harder. "I just need to find something for you to wear, honey, okay?"

I handed Brina her favorite stuffed bear and she threw it to the side. Wow, she was not in a happy mood this morning. Neither was I. I wondered if it was true that babies had a unique ability to read a person's mood. Then again, I did not think there was anyone who could *not* have felt my mood that morning.

I searched in Sabrina's closet and found a cute pair of jeans with a Notre Dame sweatshirt my sister had bought her for Christmas the previous year. It seemed warm and appropriate. I changed Brina's diaper as quickly as I could. I think I succeeded in getting her dressed faster than I had gotten myself ready. Impressive, Rose. I ran a comb through her hair, which she hated, but she looked adorable when I was finished. I decided it was time for me to finish getting ready. 7:02 a.m., I could do it. I carried my darling daughter into the master bedroom and placed her in the playpen with all her favorite toys. Nope, she was not having any of that either. So, I reverted to bribery and turned on the TV. "Please, Brina, watch the cartoons. Look how cute they are."

Just then, Xavier walked in, likely needing to get in the shower. As soon as Brina saw him, she reached for him. He said, "Sorry, baby, I need to get ready now."

Of course, that pissed her off even more, and she began crying all over again. 7:07 a.m., dammit, I needed to be getting ready. "She is just going to have to cry. I cannot pick her up right now," I said, not meaning to sound cold-hearted.

"Well, maybe you should have set the alarm like you said you would and we wouldn't be having this problem," Xavier said in a mocking tone.

"X, please, do not pin this on me. Either of us could have set it."

"Yes, but only one of us *said* we were setting it."

"Cute, shouldn't you be in the shower?" I asked with just as much sarcasm.

I attempted to dry my hair, feeling guilty the whole time because of how sad Sabrina looked in her little playpen. The guilt won me over and I decided to let her sit on my lap while I put on my makeup. Brilliant idea. I was almost ready. It was 7:18 a.m., enough time to throw on my makeup, give Brina some cereal, grab a bagel, and head out the door. However, it was not to be. Brina picked up a container of loose blush and dropped it on us both. The powder went everywhere: on her jeans, on my khakis, on my shoes. And, if I tried to rub the powder off, things only became worse.

"Aaah!" I screamed, which of course, made Brina cry. I put her back in the playpen and quickly found myself another pair of pants and shoes. Xavier came out of the shower and said, "Wait, weren't you wearing something different before?"

"Don't ask," I replied. "I have to change Sabrina's pants and then head out. She will have to eat something at Mia's house."

"Okay, I am going to try to run out of here soon too."

"Bye, love you. Sorry it was a crappy morning," I said, hoping it would all be forgotten by the evening.

"Bye, I love you too," Xavier said to the back of my head as I was already moving to take Brina to her room.

I changed her pants, grabbed a granola bar, strapped Sabrina into her car seat, and finally got in my black BMW SUV. 7:34 a.m., not too shabby. Whew, I only hoped the day would get better.

I was flying through the back door of my clinic by 8:03 a.m. As I dropped my bag behind my desk, Ally, my medical assistant, was walking in my office.

She said, "You are pretty booked today, but your 8 o'clock appointment rescheduled. So, you have some breathing time until 8:30."

As it turned out, I could have taken my time after all. At least I could say maybe the day was taking a turn for the better. I text messaged Xavier, "First patient cancelled, of course. Good luck at your meeting. Going to finally get some coffee. Sorry again. Love you." I had time to go through some phone messages and mail while drinking my coffee before my first patient, Hope Shields, arrived.

Hope Shields was one of my favorite patients. She had recently turned 18 years of age, which meant she would likely not be my patient for much longer. I met Hope when she was 15-years-old and admitted to Children's Hospital. Her chief complaints had been cough and chest pain. I remembered walking into her ER room and meeting her for the first time. Her eyes had drifted from the TV, straight to mine. She locked them there for just a moment, sizing me up. I guess I passed the test, however quick it was, because she smiled and said, "Are you my doctor? Because you look more like one of my classmates than a doctor." I liked her immediately. Anyone who thought I looked younger than my years had to be pretty amazing.

She was diagnosed with pneumonia and an empyema, which meant the space around her right lung had become filled with infected fluid. She required oxygen and antibiotics in the hospital for two weeks. I cared for her throughout her hospitalization, and we developed a strong bond. She was in high school at the time, and tried to keep up with her schoolwork while in the hospital. I was impressed right off the bat. Most kids would take the opportunity while in the hospital to slack on their homework. Hope, on the other hand, worked even harder just to keep up. I would occasionally sit in her room and help with her homework – especially Algebra, one of my specialties from my teaching days.

I learned that Hope had a complicated social situation. She had been born to a teenage mother and an abusive father – not a good combination. Hope was raised by extended family throughout her early life, although her mother tried to maintain custody. Hope had previously been admitted to Children's Hospital at the age of seven for a broken arm and multiple fractured ribs. When she presented to the emergency room, her parents reported she had fallen off of her bike. However, X-rays at the time depicted old rib fractures in various stages of healing. A physical exam revealed multiple bruises that could not be explained by a fall from a bike. Child Protective Services became involved and she was removed from her parents. Other family members were unwilling to take care of her. She entered the foster care system after that hospitalization.

Finally, at age 12, Hope found a foster family that fit. She was happy at her foster home and she was officially adopted at age 14. The Shields' family had five other adopted children and took care of four medically complex foster children. Needless to say, Hope's house was busy, but at least she was happy. She told me she loved her adoptive family, but she always wished she had more stability in her early life. I would tell her over and over how well she had turned out. She had really grown to be a wonderful young woman. Yet, she seemed to have a hard time seeing that. She once said to me, "I wish my parents had put me up for adoption when I was a baby. Maybe my life would have been better all along. There are many wonderful families looking to adopt babies. It gets harder when you get older. Trust me."

I kept thinking what an amazing girl she was, given her circumstances. We had gotten along so well during her hospital stay she decided to see me as her general pediatrician. I followed her in my resident clinic, and after completing residency, in my own pediatrics practice.

Hope was one of those patients who always made my day, both during her hospitalization and when she came to clinic. Hunter had been the same way. Whether walking in Hunter's room, seeing his eyes open and glitter, or walking in Hope's room, sharing an entertaining conversation, it was a pleasure. Hope also had striking blue eyes, as sparkling as Hunter's. Her eyes seemed to hold something deeper. She was always thinking and very quick to ask the questions on her mind. She definitely had a way of keeping me on my toes.

Over the years, she had been doing so well, I only saw her in clinic for the typical teenage issues – acne, sore throat, and school physicals. She still lived with her adoptive family, but was beginning to feel very independent. She would be heading off to college in the fall and had decided to schedule a physical exam ahead of time so she could travel during her summer vacation. Hope would be starting as a pre-med major, which of course, made me very proud. I had told her life would be hard enough in college, so she might as well enjoy her summer. She was going to perform volunteer work in South America and wanted to update her immunizations. She was one of those teenagers; she had her head on straight and gave you hope in the future. If Sabrina grew up to be exactly like her, I would be a lucky mother.

So, needless to say, I was looking forward to seeing Hope that morning. When Ally brought me her chart, I was thinking, "I know if anyone can turn my day around, it is Hope." If only I knew her visit would not only turn my day around, but would also throw everything for a loop.

I opened the exam room door and found exactly what I expected – a huge smile and shining, blue eyes. Hope leapt off the table and hugged me. I hugged back and asked how she was doing.

She replied, "I have been okay. A little tired lately, but good. Excited for the summer, that's for sure. My parents are worried about me going to South America, but I will be with a volunteer group from church. I could not be more excited!"

I said, "You look good. Your hair has gotten so long since I saw you last. I really like it. And, don't worry; you are going to have an amazing time in South America, I am sure. We will try to get you ready from a medical standpoint today, sound good?"

She said, "Sounds perfect. How have you been? How is Sabrina?"

As I said, Hope and I had gotten to know each other pretty well through the years. She had even babysat for Sabrina when Mia, our nanny, had been unavailable. "Sabrina is fabulous, getting big. You should stop by sometime to visit. She would love to see you. I have been good too. Busy, but good. So, we should get started. Given this is your physical, I want to start with a review of systems and get an overall picture of how you are doing."

"Okay, I'm ready," she replied with a smile.

"Just answer yes or no and then I will clarify anything I have questions about as we go. Any headaches recently?"

"Occasionally, but not any more than my usual," she responded.

"Blurry vision?"

"No."

"Dizziness?"

She scrunched up her nose with that question. "Well, a little, actually. I think it is probably just stress or hunger. But, I have felt a bit dizzy when I wake up in the mornings."

"Like the room is spinning or like you are light-headed?" I asked, trying to clarify.

"Like lightheaded, a little off-balance and a little nauseous at the same time."

"Hmm, you mentioned feeling more tired. Is it overall fatigue or like you want to go to sleep?"

She replied, "More fatigue, like my body just cannot keep up right now."

"Any cold symptoms: runny nose, cough, or sore throat?"

"Nope."

"Any fevers?"

"No, I don't think so."

"Any nausea, vomiting, or diarrhea?"

"No diarrhea," she answered, seeming to avoid the rest of the question.

"Okay, you already said you feel a little nauseous when you wake up, have you vomited at all?" I asked.

"Only once, two days ago. But, I had not eaten dinner the night before, so I attributed it to that."

"You have always had abnormal eating patterns. I do not remember you vomiting in the past."

"I know. I did find it a little funny," she said with a waver in her voice.

"Is there anything you are worried about in particular, Hope? You can tell me, you know."

"I know, no, I don't think so. I mean, the normal things. But, nothing new. No, nothing new. Well, no, not really." That seemed like a whole lot of "no's" when one "no" would have sufficed.

"Okay, I will take that as a no," I continued. "Have you been having any joint pains?"

"No, not that I can remember."

"Have your periods been normal since I saw you last?"

"Yep. No problem."

"When was your last menstrual cycle?"

"Umm, a couple weeks ago."

"Do you remember when?"

"Like around New Year's, I think."

"It is mid-February, so is your period late?"

"No, maybe I am just calculating wrong."

Hope had always been honest with me. She had a serious boyfriend the year before and we had talked about birth control. She told me that she was not going to have sex until she was 100% sure she was ready. She said she would come in for an appointment if she ever decided it was time. She had never made that appointment.

I asked, "How have things been going with Trent?" Trent was the "love of her life" or so she had said. I was slightly worried something might be wrong in paradise. She had been in the office for 15 minutes and had not mentioned his name.

"He broke up with me. Said he was not in love with me. Said he could not wait anymore," she said quickly, holding back tears.

"Oh, Hope, I am so sorry. Why didn't you tell me? You know I am here if you ever need to talk."

"I know, but it just happened a few weeks ago. I knew I was already coming to this appointment, so I figured we could talk now. It sucked, Rose. He broke my heart. I have been a mess since."

"I hate to bring this up, but given the symptoms you have mentioned, I have to be a good doctor and ask. Is there any chance you might be pregnant?"

She replied, "No, I told you he broke up with me because he was sick of waiting. Trent and I still had not had sex."

"Okay, I had to ask. Has anything else changed recently that might explain your symptoms?"

"Well, I will not lie to you, Rose. I have been to a few parties the last few weeks, and I drank alcohol. Not too much, but more than I ever have. I was so upset about Trent. I know it is a stupid reason."

"We have talked about it before, Hope. You have always been a brilliant girl. You know your limits, but you have to be careful. You need to know that you are in control of yourself. I want to know you are safe."

"I have been careful, I think. But, I know I need to be smarter." She started to cry.

"Oh, Hope." I walked over and hugged her. "Senior year of high school is never easy. You have always ended up on your feet before. I am here for you, but I am also willing to set you up with a counselor if you think that might help."

"Maybe, but I really feel comfortable talking to you, if that is okay?" She asked.

"Of course that is okay. While we talk, I will do your physical exam, if you are ready?"

We continued to talk about Trent and her other friends. She explained that Trent was already dating another girl in her class. Guys were such jerks. Nothing had changed since I was in high school, clearly. Overall, her physical exam was normal. Her lungs sounded clear and I did not feel anything in her abdomen that could explain the nausea and vomiting. I performed a breast exam, given her age, and the only notable finding was she winced a bit during the exam. I asked, "Is that painful?"

She replied, "A little. But that is probably a sign my period is coming."

"Okay. Well, things look good. I am slightly concerned by the group of symptoms you are endorsing. I would like to run some labs. For girls your age, I usually check a complete blood count, to make sure you are not anemic, electrolytes, to make sure you are well-hydrated, thyroid studies, given you have been more tired lately, a urinalysis, and I would usually run a pregnancy test. Are those all okay with you?"

"I do not know why you would run a pregnancy test, but other than that, sounds good," Hope said skeptically.

"Please believe me. I trust you, but it would make me feel better if we check a pregnancy test," I said, trying to reassure her.

"Umm, okay. But, unless it is an immaculate conception, it's going to be negative."

"Can you give a urine sample and then walk down to the lab for the blood work?"

"Sure, I will try not to flash anyone as I walk by."

"You can get dressed first, even though that gown is quite becoming," I said with a smile.

"Oh yeah, can I please borrow it for the prom?"

"Sure, they also come in green, if your friends are interested," I said, laughing.

I decided to see my next patient, a two-year-old with a cough, while Hope had her lab work done. I diagnosed a viral upper respiratory infection in the little boy, and headed back to my office. Ally was already in there waiting for me. She said, "Umm, Rose, I dipped Hope's urine."

I replied, "Okay, so?"

She said, "She's pregnant."

My stomach dropped. I had a mix of emotions run through me. I was sad Hope had lied to me, hurt she had not confided in me, mad at whatever boy did this, and hesitant to tell her the news. She had her whole life ahead of her. She had so many plans. She was born to a teenage mother, and now she was going to be one. This was likely going to be one of the hardest conversations I was ever going to have with a patient, and this was a patient I cared for very much.

I thanked Ally and asked her to give me a few minutes. I sat at my desk trying to think of the best way to tell Hope. She must have some inkling that this was a possibility, right? She was a very smart girl. She was going to be a pre-med major, so she had to know the signs of pregnancy. She was also only 18-years-old. She probably wanted to believe the signs pointed to anything but pregnancy. I was hoping Trent would be the man I had always heard about and not another typical teenager.

I walked slowly to Hope's exam room, took a deep breath, and knocked on the door. I was still nervous as I entered her room. I had always been up-front with Hope. I had never kept anything from her, even when she was 15 and in the hospital. This was not the time to start. I looked her straight in her blue eyes, as she had with me all those years ago. She looked right back at me, and her beautiful eyes immediately filled with tears. Before I had the chance to get a word out, she said, "I'm pregnant, aren't I?"

I nodded my head. She spoke quickly, "I am sorry I lied to you. Well, actually, I didn't really lie. Trent and I never had sex. It was at a party. I was there with a friend and a whole bunch of people I didn't know. I was drinking. I was so stupid. I wanted to do anything to hurt Trent. This guy, Max, was paying attention to me. He took me upstairs. We had sex. I wanted it at the time. I was so stupid. God, I don't know anything about him. I don't even know his last name. Shit, Rose, what am I going to do?"

By this point, my eyes were also tearing up. I was at a loss for words, which so rarely happened. Hope's whole life had just changed. She was still so innocent, sitting there on my exam table. I wanted to hug her and make it all go away, but that was not in my power, as a doctor or a friend.

I said, "First off, I want to stop hearing the word *stupid*. We both know that is not true. You are brilliant. I will need to refer you to an obstetrician and gynecologist, or what we call an Ob/Gyn. I have a friend from residency that I trust completely. Her name is Lucy Brinker. You will love her. We need to talk about this, Hope. We need to discuss your options."

She said, with the most mature voice I had ever heard come from her mouth, "There are no options.

I am having the baby. I am giving it up for adoption. I will not make this baby go through what I went through. I love it 100% already. I want what is best. I will never stop loving it, but I have made my decision."

"Hope, this is a huge decision, and you have time. You would never do to your baby what was done to you. You know I will support you, no matter what. And, the way you look right now shows me that you mean everything you are saying, but just know, you have time."

"Thank you, Rose. But, my mind is made up. I hate that I even need to make this decision. But, it is what it is. I made my bed, right? I need to take the consequences. Not that I consider the baby a consequence. It is a gift. But, it is a gift I plan to share with a family who needs a child. You may think I am sounding like it is an easy decision. It is not easy. It is difficult as hell; trust me. However, I already love the baby more than I love myself. I will give it up for adoption."

I was mesmerized. The radiance that came from her dark blue eyes as she spoke was breathtaking. She had a smile on her face. It was a smile of resolve. I got chills listening to her. She was so sure. She was stronger than so many people I knew. And, the funniest part was, I believed her 100%. I was going to be there with her the whole way.

We talked for a while longer. She sat with me while I called Lucy personally and set up Hope's first prenatal appointment. Hope asked if I would come with her and I promised I would. I asked if she needed me while she talked to her parents, but she said she could handle it and I believed her. We planned to see each other at her appointment on the 20th. I hugged her goodbye, tighter than I ever had before.

As I drove home, my phone rang. It was Samantha Wilson. I answered saying, "Hey, Sam. How are you?"

"Good good. How are you?"

"Busy, crazy day, but I am hanging in there."

"Just calling to see if you wanted to get together sometime soon. Jon has been complaining that we never see you. And, I would love to see you, and play with Sabrina," she said.

"Oh, so you are inviting yourselves over to our house, huh?"

"I didn't say that. It is not my fault that you don't like bringing Brina over here because you have to lug ten bags of toys and supplies with you," Sam replied sarcastically.

"Ha-ha. Well, why don't you both come over for dinner on the 20th? I am going to have a busy day that day and will need the relaxation. I will have X cook something on the grill."

"Well, gee, I thought you would never ask. We can be there by 6:30, if that's okay?" she asked.

"Perfect. See you then. Bring some beer, okay?"

"Will do. Never leave home without it, right?"

"I hope you do, sometimes! I miss you, Sam. Cannot wait to see you!"

"Me too. Love you, Rose."

"Love you, too."

It was an amazing part of my friendship with the Wilsons. Given everything that had happened, we never felt odd sharing our emotions. We were always honest and it was easy to tell each other our feelings. I loved that about us, and I have Hunter to thank for that wonderful part of our friendship.

When I got home that night, I headed straight to Xavier's arms. It seemed the events of the morning had been forgiven and forgotten. Sabrina was sitting on the floor playing with a puzzle. She looked up and said, "Mama." For some reason, I had a flash-back to the email from Sam years ago about Hunter first saying "Mama." Funny how things rushed back like that. I told Xavier all the basics about Hope's situation, and let him know about the Wilsons' dinner with us on the 20th. Then, I poured myself a glass of wine and sat down on the floor to play with my daughter while my husband made dinner. All things considered, it was a crazy day, but pretty close to perfect too.

❧ Chapter Fifteen ❧

The morning of February 20th went much more smoothly than that of the 17th. I dropped Sabrina at Mia's early and made it to clinic with plenty of time to spare. I rescheduled a few of my patients at the end of the day because I needed to make it to Hope's appointment with Lucy. It meant I had to work through my lunch hour, but I was willing to do it to be with Hope.

The day went by with very few glitches. I did have one slightly neurotic mother who believed a pimple on her daughter's cheek was some sort of flesh-eating bacteria. She brought articles from the internet to back her case. I had to take a little extra time to talk with her and assure her it was simply acne and not to be concerned. I finally had her walking out the door at 3:25 p.m., still with enough time to make it to Hope's appointment at 4:00 p.m. Samantha and Jonathan were going to be at our house by 6:30, so I wanted to check in with Xavier while I drove to Lucy's office.

He answered, "Hey, Babe. How was your day?"

"So far, so good. A few crazy parents, but you know, it comes with the territory. Did you pick up Sabrina?"

"Yep. She is pretty pooped today. She might actually nap while I get dinner ready. Jon called me earlier and said they would bring beer and dessert," Xavier informed me.

"Great. Hopefully Lucy is running on time. I will try to get home by 6:30. If I am a little late, hang out, serve drinks, and play with Brina. No drinks for Brina though. You know how she gets on alcohol," I joked.

"Ha-ha. Oh yes, our little boozer." He was referring to an incident the previous week when Gil was visiting and left his glass of beer on the coffee table. Before we noticed, Brina had picked it up and taken a sip. Needless to say, she cried because she did not like it. She acted funny the rest of the night, a bit unsteady on her feet. We joked she was drunk, although I know she could not have been.

I changed the subject and said, "I hope things go well today for Hope. I know she is nervous. She talked to her parents yesterday, and they were incredibly supportive. Unfortunately, her summer plans have been nipped in the bud, but she seems to be holding up well. She plans to take community college classes in the fall until the baby is born. Then, she will start at the university in January. I am telling you, X, she really has this all figured out. How she already determined all of that in two days amazes me. I could learn from her."

"Yeah, when you were pregnant with Brina, you were all over the place. Like your brain checked out when your belly got big."

"Gee, thanks, honey. Well, I am almost at Lucy's. I better call Hope and let her know I am close. I do not want her to worry."

"Okay. See you soon. I will entertain until you get here. Say 'hi' to Hope for me. Tell her to stop by some time. I would love to see her."

"Of course you would. You have always thought she was cute," I said with a giggle.

"Whoa, there. She is only 18, Babe. I do not swing that way, but her black hair and blue eyes are quite intriguing, I must say."

"I know, honey. It is okay. She is attractive. Well, on that note, I will see you soon. Love you."

"Love you, too. Bye," he replied.

I pulled into the office parking lot a few minutes before 4:00 p.m. I saw Hope's red Volkswagen bug a few cars down. Hope looked up as soon as I opened the office door. I walked over to the chair where she was sitting and enveloped her in a hug. She said, "I am glad you are here. There are so many questions on this form and I feel awful for not knowing the answers."

"I brought some of the records you asked me to bring. So, I have your immunization history and all that good stuff."

"Oh, fabulous. Those were some of the questions I did not know." She continued to diligently fill out the forms with the new information I brought from the office.

"Rose, can I be honest with you?" Hope asked suddenly.

"Of course, what is it?"

"There are a whole bunch of questions about the baby's father. I know nothing. I feel so stupid for not knowing."

"Do not use that word. I thought we had this conversation a few days ago. I do not like the word stupid. It is what it is, Hope. I am here with you and trust me when I say that Lucy is not one to judge. She is one of the most open-minded, amazing people..." My speech ended abruptly when the door leading to the back office flew open and Lucy exclaimed, "Oh my god, Rose! Come here and give me a hug!"

I had missed Lucy. I promised I would see her more often once Sabrina was born, but of course, life had gotten in the way. During residency, she was one of those new doctors who never seemed to get tired. Lucy was an African American woman, standing six feet, two inches tall, with a beautiful complexion and the energy level of a two-year-old. I was always jealous of her. Ob/Gyn residency had worse call hours than we did in Pediatrics, and yet, she did not show it. She could run a marathon post-call, and I was known to fall asleep at the dinner table. It must have been her years as a college basketball player that helped. Too bad my basketball career ended in high school, if you could call riding the bench much of a career at all. Lucy and I hugged and shared some quick words, and then I introduced her to Hope.

"Lucy, I would like you to meet my favorite patient, Hope. You better take care of her. You took care of me when I was pregnant, so I know you can handle her."

"If I handled you and your insane hormones, I can take on anything!" Lucy said with a laugh.

"Was I really that bad when I was pregnant? Xavier said something along the same lines today."

"No, honey," chimed Lucy. "You were just pregnant."

She continued, "So, Hope, you are as charming as described. Let's get back there and get started, okay?"

I said, "I can wait here while you two get to know each other. I will come back later for the exam and ultrasound if you want. I am your moral support, so whatever you need."

Hope replied, always with more maturity than her years, "I think I can do the history part, but I am nervous about the exam. Could we call you in to hold my hand? I know it sounds stupid. Oh, I mean, it sounds silly. Sorry, Rose, no more stupid."

"Thank you. Have the nurse come and get me whenever. Lucy, behave yourself."

I sat in the waiting room reading a parenting magazine. God, just being in the office made me want to have a baby. I thought to myself, "I better not drink from the water fountain; pregnancy may be contagious around here."

I was busy reading and thinking about Hope and her little one when April, one of the nurses I knew from my pregnancy, called my name. We shared pleasantries as we headed to Hope's room. When I walked in, Hope's blue eyes appeared a bit frightened. "Oh, Hope, what's wrong?"

"I have never had an exam like this before. It grosses me out, honestly. Please tell me some funny story while she checks, okay?"

"I will, and I promise Lucy is the best there is. So, you have nothing to worry about." I chose to tell her the story of Brina and the beer since it was fresh in my mind. It was a hit. The exam was over before Hope knew it.

Lucy announced, "Now, for the big part. I know you are planning to give your baby up for adoption. I am assuming you would still like to see the ultrasound. Some mothers feel it is too emotional for them."

"I can handle it. I have told Rose already. I love this baby. I want to be a part of all of this. It will not change my mind. It will only make my conviction stronger that I want what is best for him or her. I am assuming it is too early to tell which, right?"

"Oh, darling," said Lucy, "when you see how much it looks like a teddy graham cracker, you will know it is way too early to tell."

"Wow, great, I am having a teddy bear for a baby! I might have to go to the zoo to find the adoptive parents," Hope replied with her sense of humor still intact.

"Didn't I tell you, Lucy?" I stated. "She has our sense of humor."

Lucy was still laughing as she rolled in the ultrasound machine. When she got everything situated, an image began to form on the screen. Sure enough, it was a teddy graham, if you could even call it that. But, it was remarkable. I saw at least one tear form in Hope's dark blue eyes, as I felt one drip down my own cheek. Lucy pointed out the important features, including the rapid motion of the beating heart. In that moment, Hope's face lit up into a beautiful smile, still with the glint of happy tears in her eyes. Lucy did some measurements and said, "From the looks of things, you conceived about six weeks ago."

"Well, seeing as I had sex one time in my whole life, I could pin it down to more like the minute I conceived. It was January 14th at about 11:15 p.m. He didn't last very long. Guess I just turned him on too much. Sorry, guys. I should not joke about it. But, Rose can tell you, it is my defense mechanism."

"I am not easily offended," I said. "And, trust me; no one has a stranger sense of humor than Lucy."

"Thanks, Rose. I will take that as a compliment." Lucy printed a picture of the ultrasound saying to Hope, "You can keep this or pass it along to the adoptive parents."

"Print two. One for me and one for them."

"What about me?" I asked. "Come on, I am going to be the Lamaze coach."

"Sorry, Rose. Of course. One more for Rose," Hope said.

Lucy and I chatted in the hallway while Hope got dressed. Lucy started, "Wow, you were right. This girl is unbreakable. She knows what she wants. What an amazing girl she is!"

"Tell me about it. I want her to spend more time with Brina. Maybe some of it will rub off."

"I wish I could have her give a seminar to some of my other teenage moms. She would be great," Lucy said.

"She would probably do it, too, if you asked," I replied.

Hope walked out and smiled, thanking Lucy for everything. Another appointment was set for the following month. We made sure it was a day and time I could be there. I hugged Lucy "goodbye" and we promised to see each other socially some time soon. As we walked out, Lucy called after us, "Tell Xavier 'hi' for me and kiss that little Sabrina too."

"Will do. Bye, Lucy," I replied.

By the time we made it out to the cars, I looked down at my watch and realized it was already 6:00 p.m. Wow, time had flown. I was at least a half hour from home and knew Jon and Sam would be prompt as always. While I was hugging Hope in the parking lot, her phone rang. She picked up and was clearly talking to Louisa, her adoptive mother. She told her quickly about the appointment and then hung up.

Hope said to me, "Well, I guess I am on my own for dinner. That was my mom saying the rest of the family is ordering in pizza now. By the time I get there, it will be pretty picked over, I am sure."

"You are not eating on your own after a big day like today. You are coming over and having dinner with us. We are having some friends over that I have known a little longer than I have known you. You will love them! Xavier was saying he has not seen you and I am sure Sabrina would be thrilled to have you there. I will not take 'no' for an answer."

"Well, I guess my decision is made then. I would love to see Xavier and Sabrina. You are way too sweet to me. Thank you."

"It is our pleasure. I will let Xavier know to put another steak on the grill."

"Okay, I think I remember how to get to your house, but I will follow you just in case."

"Sounds good. See you there. Drive safe. You are carrying precious cargo, you know?"

"Oh, trust me, I know. I vomited again this morning. The little teddy graham just keeps on reminding me." We both laughed.

I waited for Hope to join me in my driveway before walking into the house. Jon's truck was already there and it was only 6:33 p.m. on my car's clock. Hope walked towards me saying, "Are you sure this is okay? Your friends are probably going to feel that I am intruding on their time with you."

"Trust me. Jon and Sam are two of the most understanding people you will ever meet. You have nothing to worry about. And, plus, if they have a problem, I will have to kick their asses." She laughed as I unlocked the front door.

I forgot to warn Hope about Tucker and Jake's onslaught when I returned from work. I had to blockade her before they made a beeline and jumped up on her pregnant stomach. "Tucker and Jake, stay down. Hope is excited to see you, but you cannot jump."

Sabrina came waddling into the hallway behind the dogs. She looked up at Hope with a sense of recognition. It had probably been four or five months since she had seen her. To a 17-month-old, it must have seemed like a lifetime. I greeted her, "Hi, baby. I missed you. This is Hope. You used to play with her. Do you remember?"

She looked at me with a confused hint in her brown eyes. She said, "Play?" I figured that was a good sign. Hope took her hand and walked into the family room. Sam and Jon were sitting on the couch and I waved to Xavier who was hard at work on the grill.

Sam and Jon both got up to greet me with big hugs and kisses. As Sabrina was showing Hope one of her favorite baby dolls, I said, "Samantha and Jonathan, I would like you to meet one of my favorite patients, and one of my friends, Hope Shields. Hope, these are two of my dearest friends, Samantha and Jonathan Wilson."

They shared handshakes and already had smiles on their faces. Hope said, "God, I cannot believe how big Sabrina is. She is beautiful, Rose. She definitely has your eyes."

I replied, "I know, X always says he wishes she got his blue eyes. He claims he had to *settle* for brown."

"I never said settle," Xavier said as he walked in the back door. "I love everything about her. And, I am sure one of our future children is bound to get my eyes. As long as they have your brains, babe."

"Oh, too sweet." I walked over and kissed him. Hope also snuck away from Sabrina for a moment to say "hi" to Xavier and give him a hug. He winked at me over her shoulder.

"Can I get you two ladies a drink?" Jon asked while walking to get another beer from the kitchen.

"I would love a beer," I replied. "Hope, on the other hand, is not of age for a beer."

"And, I happen to be pregnant, but I would love an ice water. Thanks," she said, matter-of-factly. I did not want to be the one to bring up the pregnancy in front of people she had just met.

Sam chimed in from the couch, "You look 21, Hope. I never would have guessed younger."

Hope said, "Yep, I am only 18 and a senior in high   school."

"You must be mature for your years," Sam said. "How have you been feeling? How far along are you?"

Hope replied, "I am feeling okay, I guess. Still getting used to the whole thing. I have been dealing with a bit of morning sickness. And, to answer your other question, I am only a little more than one month along."

Sam said, "I figured you were early on. You are not showing at all. But, you will probably be the lucky one who keeps her looks and her figure for the whole nine months, unlike Rose and me."

"Hey," I said, "speak for yourself. I was hot when I was pregnant."

"Hot and 30 pounds heavier," Jon stated while handing me a beer.

"Now I see why Sam occasionally has to put you in your place," I joked while punching him playfully on the arm.

Hope sat down on the floor to play with Sabrina, getting tackled by Tucker and Jake in the meantime. "X, maybe we need to let Tucker and Jake out to run in the backyard for a bit. They are going to kill someone."

Xavier called the dogs and ran with them outside. Hope said, "Sam, you said you gained weight in your pregnancy. Is the baby here sleeping somewhere?"

Oops, I probably should have let Hope know about Hunter ahead of time, but again, I did not know if it was my place to say something. Sam looked at Jon, took a deep breath, and said, "Hunter was our little boy. But, umm, he is not here right now. Actually, he passed away a few years back."

"Oh my god. I am so sorry for both of you," Hope said, her eyes wet with tears. "I am sorry I asked. I did not know."

"It is okay. We have talked about it a lot over the years. He was our angel. Perfect in every way. You do not know how lucky you are. The morning sickness and the weight gain do not matter at all. When you look in your baby's eyes, you will forget everything else," Sam said to Hope.

"I am sure I will. But, given my age and all, I should tell you, I am giving my baby up for adoption. I know I am not prepared to care for a baby right now. I am starting college. There has to be some wonderful couple looking to adopt a baby."

"Oh, I am sorry," Sam said, "I should not have made an assumption."

"Not at all," Hope replied. "I am looking forward to the whole process actually. I will take any advice you have to offer. I am also looking forward to giving my baby as a gift to some family."

"We have started some of the paperwork for adoption ourselves on the other side of things. Just so you know to be careful because there are many loopholes. Make sure you have someone good looking out for you on your end," Jon stated.

"Jenica is going to help Hope through the process. I know she will look out for Hope and the baby. We are only a few days into all this, so we still have time," I relayed to them.

"Jenica is fabulous. You are in good hands," Sam said. "She has been helping us out as well."

Xavier returned from outside with the steaks sizzling on a plate and said, "Well, not to break up the conversation, but dinner is pretty much ready if you all want to move into the dining room. Come on, Brina; let's get you in your high chair."

"K, Dada."

We filed into the dining room, ready for good food and good company. We sat down and the conversation began flowing easily. Sam and Jon filled us in on their family members. Jon said, "I talked to Nanny and Poppy today. They send their love. They wanted to know when you two are going to bring Sabrina to visit so they can meet her."

"Well, we should probably take her to Pittsburgh sometime soon to visit my extended family.

Maybe we will hit up all of Pennsylvania while we are there," I replied.

Sam asked how my family was doing. I told her that Kyle and Prilla were still going strong and doing well. She asked when they were going to get engaged. I said, "It cannot happen soon enough in my mind. I love her."

I told them Jenica, Tim and the triplets were doing well. Sam could not believe they were almost going to be three-years-old. Sam and Jon had seen my parents at our last dinner together in January. We had met my mom and dad at a steak restaurant recommended by one of my patients. I said, "I talked to my parents today. They send their love to you both. And, Hope, I am sure they would send their love to you, too."

"They have never met me," she said questioningly.

"Well, I guarantee they would love you the second they met you. They are both good judges of character," I replied.

There was a bit of a lull in the conversation as everyone enjoyed the steak and trimmings. Hope looked up with that glint of curiosity in her blue eyes. "I am sorry to ask, but ever since you brought it up, I have not been able to get it out of my mind. Samantha, do you mind if I ask what happened to your son?"

"I do not mind at all. Rose may be able to give you the medical details better, though, if I mess up. Hunter was diagnosed with mitochondrial DNA depletion syndrome. From my understanding and all my reading, it means he had almost no energy-making cells in his body. His muscles did not work right, and his liver and brain suffered most of all. When Rose first met him at Children's, he was doing relatively well, but time passed. He took a turn for the worse and died of liver failure when he was just about 11-months-old."

Hope said with true concern in her voice, "Wow, that must have been so hard for you, but I am glad Rose was your doctor. She was my doctor at Children's too. I chose to keep her as my pediatrician because I loved her so much."

Jon interjected, "That is what we did too. We requested Rose on Hunter's last admission. She had taken care of him on his first trip to Children's, and she was his doctor when he died. We would not have wanted it any other way."

"Stop, guys, you are making me blush," I said.

"Sure we are. You love this stuff!" Jon said with a sparkle in his eyes.

Hope then said, "Can I ask one more personal question since we are all friends now?"

"Of course," Jon and Sam said in unison.

"Why adoption? Why not try to have another child?"

Jon answered, "The doctors think Hunter's problem was genetic. We would run the risk of having another baby with the same thing. Sam and I loved Hunter more than life itself. When he died, a part of us died too. We could not put ourselves through that again. Plus, Hunter suffered. We could not put another baby through the same pain. Until there are other scientific options, we are content with adoption. It doesn't mean we are closing off to future kids of our own, though."

By that time, Jon's eyes were full of tears, as were the rest of the eyes around the table. "Sorry to put such a damper on things," Hope said.

"No, we usually end up crying when we are together," I said. "We all miss Hunter, and he seems to always end up the center of conversation. In eleven months, that baby made a whole lot of lovely memories."

"Wait," Hope said quickly. "Was Hunter the baby whose picture was on the back of your badge when I was a patient at Children's?"

"Yes. Good memory," I said. "You were admitted probably five or six months after he was there. And, come to think of it, weren't you in room 2026?"

"I think so."

"That is ironic," I spoke. "2026 was Hunter's room, the room in which he passed away."

"Wow, sometimes, it is such a small world. Now, we are all sitting here eating dinner, talking about Hunter. That little guy keeps on bringing people together," Xavier said, so poignantly.

We continued to share Hunter stories throughout the rest of the meal. Hope and the Wilsons seemed like old friends by the end of dinner. I was not surprised. Good people seemed to get along well with each other. Hope asked a list of questions about pregnancy. Sam and I gave her honest responses, but kept some things to ourselves so she did not get too worried. Sam winked at me while she said, "Childbirth is a piece of cake. Women are strong. If Rose and I survived, you will too!"

☙☙☙❧❧❧

Time seemed to fly by and we moved to the family room sometime in the middle of a conversation between Jon and Xavier about the Super Bowl. While we sat talking and laughing, Sabrina fell asleep in my arms. That seemed to be the cue to us that we were getting tired. Sam said, "Well, we better get going. We do have a bit of a drive ahead of us."

"I should get going, too. I have class in the morning," Hope stated next.

"Oh my goodness. I am a bad doctor. I kept you up past your bedtime."

"Shut up, Rose. It is only 9:30," Hope said with a wink in my direction. "I will be okay, but I should probably get to driving."

I set Sabrina down on the couch, where she curled up in a ball. We shared hugs as we said goodbye. Sam and Jon wished Hope luck with the pregnancy and school. Hope thanked them for sharing their experiences about Hunter. As Jon climbed in his truck, he said, "Hey Rose, you can invite Hope whenever we hang out. She is an amazing girl."

"I know how to pick my favorite patients, I guess!" I said, referring to Hope and Hunter.

"Well, I would love to see you again, too," Hope responded with a smile on her face.

Xavier and I continued to wave as they pulled out of the driveway. "We are pretty lucky to have such wonderful people in our lives," I said to him.

"As you always say, we are already blessed with terrific families. We are *extra*-blessed to have friends who are also remarkable."

I agreed, saying, "There was something in the air when we were together. I think tonight worked out exactly as it was supposed to."

"I agree. It was a really nice evening."

"And, the steak was fabulous, too. Thank you," I said to Xavier as I kissed him on the cheek and walked inside to take our darling daughter to bed.

᠙ Chapter Sixteen ᠙

Hope's next prenatal appointment with Lucy arrived quickly. According to Lucy, everything was progressing nicely. The morning sickness had almost resolved, so Hope was feeling better as well. After the appointment, I asked if Hope wanted to spend some time together and get a pedicure. I said, "I would love to take this opportunity to have some girl time. Are you up for it? My treat."

"That sounds like a great idea. For as many times as I am going to be gowning up and spreading my legs, I figure my toes should at least be cute."

"Well, or you could get a Brazilian wax or something," I joked.

"I think I will settle for a pedicure," Hope replied.

"Let's do it," I said.

As we sat with our feet in the hot swirling tubs, I felt relaxed. We both read trashy magazines and shared fun tips with each other as we found them. We laughed and had a wonderful time. As I was caught up in the fifth article in one magazine about

"How to Make Your Man Orgasm Every Time," I heard my name.

I looked up to see Samantha at the front desk. I asked what she was doing there. She said, "I was down here meeting up with a friend for coffee. As I drove by, I decided to treat myself to a pedicure. I must have had a sixth sense you girls would be here."

"Well, join us, please! We are having a girly-girl afternoon and reading really trashy magazines," Hope said.

"I think I will," Sam said while giving us both hugs.

As Sam got situated in her chair, Hope suddenly exclaimed, "Dr. Rose Gorman, is that a tattoo I see?" She was clearly referring to the heart on my right foot between my first and second toes.

"Why yes, it is, Hope. You seem surprised."

"Surprised to say the least. You are so straight-laced. I mean, I know the tattoo is small, but it is still a tattoo. I hope it involves some night of debauchery that you do not share with anyone," Hope said with a glint of sarcasm in her blue eyes.

"Oh yes, you know Rose. She was crazy in her younger days," Sam replied with similar inflection.

"Excuse me, I had my crazy days, Sam. Maybe I just keep my secrets to myself," I said, trying to sound cooler than I was.

"Rose, you did not have a sip of alcohol before your sophomore year of college. Trust me, there was no craziness in your *younger* days," Sam countered.

"Well, I more than made up for it in my last few years of college."

"Sure you did. At Notre Dame. Our good Catholic girl," Hope said, smiling.

"We knew how to have fun at Notre Dame. Do not judge. You are at Catholic school, too," I said with a laugh.

"That is true. You know, Sam, I might have to believe Rose. We Catholic girls do know how to party. My little baby bump here proves that," Hope stated still in good humor.

Sam said, "Hope, as much as I would love to tell you that I got Rose drunk, took her out, and made her get the tattoo, it is not the case. She did it for Hunter."

"Oh, wow, sorry I made fun of you, Rose. That is so sweet," Hope said sounding interested. "Sam, please tell me the story."

"Well, about six months after Hunter passed away, Jon's family got together for his aunt's wedding. We all planned to get tattoos in honor of Hunter. I had his name tattooed on the inside of my wrist. Jon got Hunter's picture on his forearm," Sam began.

"Oh yeah, he told me about that when I asked him at dinner the other night," Hope interjected.

"Exactly. So, the other women at the wedding got a small hunter green heart tattooed, each on her right foot. Rose was not there for the wedding, since she was here working, likely meeting you," Sam continued.

"Actually, the timing is just about right," I said.

"When we got back from the wedding, I told Rose it was her turn. She was scared to death. We kept saying she had to do it for Hunter, so she conceded. You would have thought we asked her to brand herself with a hot iron. She was petrified. She must have asked the guy at the tattoo parlor one hundred times if he sterilized the needle. She asked for health department documentation. It was a bit embarrassing."

"I have seen enough Hepatitis C in my day to be careful," I countered.

"You are such a doctor, Rose," Hope said with a wink.

"And proud of it," I said with my own wink.

"Well, I have to say, I was proud of Rose in the end. She got the 'hunter green' heart on her foot. Hunter would be proud," Samantha concluded.

"I am proud of you, too, Rose. You did something I never would have thought you would do. If I die, would you tattoo another heart for me?" Hope asked with a laugh.

"Don't even joke about it. But, yes, anything for you dear," I replied.

"I think I am going to get my first tattoo in honor of the baby. Since I will be giving him or her up for adoption, I want something to remember the time we spent together. Does that sound strange?" Hope pondered aloud.

"I think it would be a very sweet gesture," Sam reassured her.

"Although I am still not the biggest fan of tattoos, as long as you are careful, it might be nice for you," I said, trying not to sound like the party pooper. I knew in the back of my mind I had time to talk her out of it before the baby was born.

The afternoon only got better from there, surrounded by one of my best friends and my favorite patient. I loved hearing about Hope's high school experiences, reminded of the drama of my own high school days. Sam met Jon when she was still in high school, so she enjoyed sharing memories as well. It felt like we were the best of friends, and it proved to be exactly what we needed.

We parted ways, our feet in flip-flops to protect our beautiful toes. As we said goodbye, Sam suggested, "We should do this again sometime. It was really fun."

"It really was. I know I am only 18, but thanks for making me feel welcome," Hope said.

"God, we are not that old, but we enjoyed you being here too, Hope," I replied. We hugged and each got in our own cars. As I drove away, I realized I had missed out on having girl friends. I looked forward to the next opportunity we would have to spend time together.

It turned out I did not have to wait very long. At the end of March was Xavier's 35th birthday. He had already decided we would rent a boat on the lake for his party. He handled the logistics, and I was in charge of food, drink, and decorations. We planned to go out for a few hours on the lake, relax, and enjoy the weather.

March 20th was a sunny day with a light breeze, ideal boating weather. All the guests met at the dock, most with gifts and food or drinks to share. My entire family was able to make it, including the triplets. The three were dressed in the cutest outfits, each with matching hats and sun block on their cheeks. The boat was ready to cast off, so we began to board. Of course, we could not pull away from the dock because Jack and Melony had not yet arrived. Xavier's parents had made it and I was so glad they had come since they would be moving to California a few weeks later. I knew it meant a lot to Xavier for them to be there.

I heard my father-in-law leaving Jack a message, "I told you guys noon, and it is 12:15. It is hard to guess which one of you is running late, because you both have issues with punctuality. So, you better get your asses here as soon as possible. It is your brother's birthday and we will leave without you."

"Thanks, Dad," I heard Xavier say while helping him onto the boat. Both my mother and mother-in-law were busy talking about how cute Sabrina looked. I had to agree with them. She was wearing a little sailor sundress and a sailor hat to shade her from the sun. When I was little, I never would have kept the hat on my head, but she seemed to love it.

Jonathan and Samantha were there, as was Hope. They were so much like family now that I could not imagine a gathering without them. Plus, I hoped my family would get to know Hope a little better, since she was so important to me. Just as Xavier was about to put the boat in gear, Kyle said, "Wait, I see Melony's car pulling up."

"Oh, fine, we will wait," Xavier said, slightly perturbed.

"No, just go. It will serve them right for never being on time. They can swim to the boat," his father replied.

"Oh, Dad. Calm down. They are here. Let's be happy for that," my mother-in-law said, ever the peacemaker.

We watched as Jack pulled himself out of Melony's car. It would take him awhile to make it to the boat, given he walks slowly. We also noticed it was going to take him even longer because Melony was yelling at him and putting gifts in his arms. "Maybe I should go help them," I said, trying to move things along.

"I will come, too," Kyle said.

We both ran to where Melony and Jack were still arguing. "Hey, you two. Can we help?" I asked.

"Oh, thank god. Rose, I just had my nails done, so I cannot carry a thing. Jack is useless. So, if you could grab the gifts, I would really appreciate it. Kyle, it is fabulous to see you and aren't you just a dear for wanting to help me. You are such a sweetheart. Could you carry the wine and the bag of my toiletries?" Melony gushed.

I whispered to Kyle under my breath as we walked ahead, "It is as if I am not even here when you are around. Maybe you two will end up together."

He whispered in return, "Come on, Rose, she is Xavier's sister, and plus, I am in love with Prilla."

At that, I paused and kissed him on the cheek. "I think I may be in love with her too. Well, at least, I am in love with the two of you together."

I looked back to see how far ahead we were. Melony was walking while applying lipstick, so she remained a few steps behind. Still only a few paces from the car, Jack asked, "Guess you don't run a tram to the boat, huh?"

"Nope, you have to walk and get your exercise. Relax when you get there," I replied, feeling the need to give my medical advice whenever I had the chance.

It took about 15 minutes, but we finally arrived on the boat and Xavier pulled away from the dock. As I arranged the food, I noticed Samantha and Hope sitting on the deck talking and laughing. It was so nice to see them getting along, since Hope only knew a few people there. Xavier's friend Gil had found Jon, and once they realized they both loved to hunt, they spent the rest of the day together, drinking beers and telling stories.

I was able to sneak to Xavier's side at one point during the day. I said, "Whew, I have been so busy, but I wanted to say, 'Happy Birthday.'"

"Thank you. This is perfect. Everyone seems to be having such a great time, especially my parents. I could not be happier." I kissed him and headed in the direction of where the kids were playing. I walked by Sam and Hope on the way overhearing them talk about Hunter. They were so deep in conversation; I did not bother to interrupt. I needed to get a few pictures of the kids before they pooped out.

The hours went by and the fun did not stop. I had a few strawberry margaritas my dad had made, and I was feeling perfectly tipsy. I noticed Melony had a few drinks as well, and she was hanging on Gil's every word. Jon had to occasionally put his arm out to keep her from getting too close to the edge of the boat, as she was slightly unsteady on her feet.

My mom, Jenica, and Prilla had found Samantha and Hope, so I decided to join them. When I arrived, Jenica was saying, "You look amazing for being pregnant. I know you are early on, but I was so sick with the triplets, I had constant bags under my eyes."

"I am very good at under-the-eye makeup," Hope replied with a smile.

"Well, Rose, Hope is just as perfect as you always described," my mom said to me.

"Oh, thank you. Rose, you always say such nice things about me. I do not know what I did to deserve you," Hope said in reply.

"You had an empyema, remember? Thank God for empyemas, I guess," I joked.

"What is an empyema?" Jenica asked.

"It is a fluid collection, oh never mind. This is a party. No medical talk. Let's just be glad I met her," I responded.

The conversation continued on for at least another 30 minutes. Jon joined in at one point when Gil went to talk with Xavier. He and Samantha could always bring such laughter to any group. I smiled so much while we talked my cheeks actually hurt. That is how I knew it was such a good day. I would glance up occasionally and catch X's eye, or look over and see Sabrina sleeping in my dad's arms while he talked with Tim. "Yes," I thought, "quite a flawless day."

We opened gifts on the boat before bringing it back to the dock. Xavier was on cloud nine. Usually as we get older, the gifts do not matter as much, but our guests did well. He received some pretty cool gifts, including a snowboard from Jenica, Tim, Kyle, Prilla, and the triplets. He had been meaning to learn for years and now he had no excuse. Along the same line, my parents gave him lift tickets to a ski resort nearby so we could go come wintertime. His parents gave him a gift card for airline flights. His dad said, "So you can visit us as soon as possible. I will miss you." This brought both X and his dad close to tears.

It took awhile to clean everything off the boat, especially with four sleeping children we were trying not to wake. But, somehow, with the extra help, we did a pretty good job. It was not until we had said our goodbyes and I was climbing in the passenger seat of the SUV, with Sabrina asleep in her car seat, I realized how insanely tired I was. "What a day, honey! I am beyond tired."

"Me, too. And it is only early evening," Xavier said.

"Well, I have always been a believer in napping whenever and wherever. You know that," I replied.

"Then, let's go nap. A family nap sounds wonderful to me. I will walk Tucker and Jake when we wake up."

All three of us only awoke from our naps long enough to walk the dogs, eat a quick dinner, get ready for bed, and climb right back in for a good night's sleep. I thought Sabrina would wake up in the middle of the night since she had napped so late in the day, but she slept straight through. I guess she had as much fun as we did, but at least there was no alcohol for her this time.

About a week later, I received a call from Samantha. As soon as I picked up the phone, she said, "Jon just won tickets on the radio to the upcoming country blow-out concert! You know, the one with about ten different bands and singers performing?"

"That is awesome, Samantha. You are going to have a blast. I am totally jealous."

"That is why I am calling, dork. He won four tickets. And, we want you and Xavier to come with us," she replied.

"Oh, wow! That is so sweet of you. When is the concert?"

"April 30th. Do you think you can make it?" She asked.

"I can be there. But, I am pretty sure that is the night X already has tickets to the baseball game. I am sure he will be so disappointed, because we know how much he loves country music," I said sarcastically.

"Oh, yeah. How could I forget about that?"

"We could always have Mia watch Sabrina and find a fourth person to join us at the concert," I said.

"How about Hope? I remember her saying she loves country music, too," Samantha considered.

"I think she would love to come. Are you sure you do not want to ask somebody else, like one of your other friends?"

"Not at all. Jon and I both love Hope. And, she could probably use the fun. She seems like she is working so hard at school right now," Sam countered.

"Okay, I will ask her. But, count me in," I replied.

It turned out Hope was free that night and she was very excited about the invitation. April 30th came quickly and we climbed into Jon's truck together to head to the concert. I had bought a cowboy hat for the occasion, which of course, made Jon and Sam laugh hysterically.

The concert was a blast and it seemed like Hope was having a wonderful time as well. The first group to perform was an up-and-coming local country band. Their last song was about friendship and the unbreakable bonds between people. When the song ended and the band headed off stage, Sam said, "That song really described us, huh? We did not really meet in conventional ways, but we sure have unbreakable bonds between us."

"I agree. It was a wonderful song," Hope responded.

"Oh, be honest, Hope. You just thought the lead singer was hot," Jon joked.

"You got me, Jon. But, so what? I am single. As long as he is okay with the pregnant belly look. Maybe he will think, 'at least she puts out.'" Hope retorted.

"Hope, stop. Any guy would be lucky to have you," I said with a smile, understanding her sense of humor.

"I know, but I can still joke about it," she said.

"Of course. Maybe we can sneak you backstage and introduce you to him," I stated.

"I met Jon at a gas station, and Rose met X at a bar, so you would be the classiest of the bunch if you met your guy backstage at a country concert," Sam said. "So, let's try."

"Let's not. Maybe next year," Hope replied.

"Okay, fine. Party pooper," Jon concluded. By that point, the next singer had taken the stage.

"Not as cute as the last one, but maybe he has a good voice," Hope said, still smiling.

The rest of the night proved to be as much fun as the beginning. On the ride home, we were exhausted, but as usual we found ourselves talking about Hunter. Hope was genuinely interested in hearing our stories and remained completely enthralled. By the time Sam and Jon dropped us off and Hope was getting in her car, I was feeling confident I had some of the best friends in the world.

❧ Chapter Seventeen ❧

As I walked out of the local drug store on the day after the concert, I could feel my phone vibrating in my purse. It was times like those I felt like Mary Poppins, as if my bag could contain a hat rack and I would not be surprised. There was no way there could possibly be so many things in my bag that I could not find my phone, especially with it vibrating. Finally, I felt my phone, pulled it out, and answered it without checking the caller ID, "Hello?"

"Rose, it is Hope."

"Hey, sweetie, is everything okay?"

"Actually, I think everything is completely perfect now."

"Okay. That makes me happy. But, why is today more perfect than yesterday?" I asked.

She said with complete happiness in her voice, "I was up all night last night and I came up with something amazing."

"Oh, so you are delirious from pregnancy hormones and loss of sleep, fabulous."

"Maybe delirious, but totally happy," Hope replied.

"Which could just be delirium," I countered.

"Oh, listen to me, Rose. I would like to ask Samantha and Jonathan if they would be the adoptive parents for my baby."

I almost dropped the phone. How had I not thought of this before with three of the most important people in my life? Maybe it seemed too good to be true, so I had put it out of my mind. But, now, hearing Hope say those words, it all made sense. My thoughts were broken by Hope's voice, "Umm. Rose? Did you hear me? Are you there?"

"Yes, yes, Hope. I heard you. I am speechless."

"Why, you think it is a bad idea? I have thought about it over and over and there are only good reasons."

"No. It is not a bad idea at all. In fact, I think it is a fabulous idea. I am a little bitter that I did not think of it."

"Well, Rose, you brought us together, so I will give you a little bit of the credit. But, just a little," she said with a laugh.

"Thanks, honey. So, what now? What are you going to do?"

"I was hoping I could call your sister and run it by her. Then, I want to set up a dinner so I can talk to Sam and Jon with you there for support. Xavier and Sabrina are welcome, too, of course. I would like to bring up the proposition in person."

"Okay. Hope, you know I have always supported you. It is really your decision, and as usual, you sound like you know what you are doing. As for dinner, I am assuming sooner is better?"

"Yes, I am super-excited. So, if all goes well with Jenica, then let's set up dinner for tomorrow night. They may think it is odd since we were together last night, but we can say you have news or something," Hope suggested.

"Okay, I can swing that. Call me after you talk to Jenica and I will set it up. Are you sure, Hope?"

"I am sure. And, I know in my heart they are the right people."

"Please do not get your hopes too high quite yet. I can only imagine they will be honored. But, just in case," I said.

"I know. I have my head on straight. You know that. I have a gut feeling. And, my gut feelings are usually right."

"Well, as long as the gut feeling is not indigestion or the baby kicking, I will believe you."

"Thanks, Rose. I hope to see you tomorrow."

"Okay, I will make reservations at the Italian restaurant we love close to our house."

"Perfect. I love you, Rose. Thank you."

"I will hope for the best. I love you, too." As I pressed the end button on my phone, I realized my palms were sweating. There was something amazing about to happen. I did not want to get her hopes up, but I also had a gut feeling this was the way things were meant to be.

According to Jenica, there would be legal paperwork and agreements she would have to assemble. There could be a few loopholes, so she warned Hope to be prepared for a few bumps in the road, but Jenica sounded like she could make things happen. I had never heard Hope as happy as when she called to pass on the information to me. Dinner was scheduled, and I could not wait. Samantha seemed sure I was pregnant again, so I tried to keep my emotions on track when I invited her to dinner. And, of course, she said, "We will be there with bells on!"

Xavier could sense my anxiety before dinner. He said, "I am sure things will go well."

"I know. I hope so. Hope is so set on it. And, I do not want Jon and Sam to feel they are in an uncomfortable situation where they have to say 'yes.'"

"I may not know them as well as you do, but the one thing I know about them is they are honest. They will do what they want to do," he replied.

"You are right. Grab Sabrina out of her playpen and let's go," I said with butterflies in my stomach.

Sabrina had grown close to Hope over the previous months, so when we walked in the restaurant, she immediately jumped out of X's arms and into Hope's. "Well, hello, Sabrina, don't you look cute tonight?" Hope asked.

"Din-din," Brina said.

"She loves the food here," I said as I kissed Hope on the cheek. "She may be a picky eater, but she sure loves Italian food."

"Just like her mother," Xavier uttered as he too kissed Hope.

"They said the table is ready. Should we sit and wait for Sam and Jon?" Hope asked.

"Sure, otherwise Sabrina will get restless," I replied.

As we sat, we left the two seats next to Hope empty so she could easily talk to both Sam and Jon. We ordered drinks, including a glass of wine for me. I needed to calm my nerves, since Hope seemed as relaxed as ever. Sam and Jon walked into the restaurant and were directed to our table. They both kissed Sabrina on the forehead, as I used to do with Hunter.

While browsing the menu and ordering our meals, the conversation varied from Hope's classes to the house Xavier sold to Sam's involvement in a charity for children with chronic illnesses. There came a point where there was a break in the conversation. Hope looked at me and I nodded, giving her the go ahead. She said, "Well, I know everyone thought we were coming here tonight for news about Rose. But, as you can tell by her second glass of wine, she is not pregnant. The truth is; I asked you to be here for what I hope to be some news of my own."

"What kind of news, Hope?" Sam asked. "Is everything okay?"

"I hope so. I better take a deep breath because I am a little nervous. Jon and Sam, the news involves you two. I have truly enjoyed the time we have spent together since I met you back in February. I feel like I have known you even longer than that. From what Rose told me before, and what I have learned on my own, I know you are both amazing people."

"Thank you, Hope. You are amazing yourself," Jon said, looking unsure of what was coming next.

"Thank you. So, here is the thing. I love my baby with all my heart. You both know that. But, I also know I am not the right parent for him or her. I want this baby to have everything, including the most loving parents around, and I think I have found those parents in the two of you."

Sam and Jon both gasped as she said those words.

Hope continued, "My question for you tonight is whether you would be willing to consider adopting my little one? I know he or she would never replace Hunter, but I know the baby would receive as much love and affection as he did. From what I have heard, that would be a whole lot. Plus, maybe I could still hear from you about how he or she is doing through the years."

By that time, both Sam and Jon had tears in their eyes, as did I. I did not know which one was going to speak first. They looked at each other, looked at me, and then looked back at Hope. Finally, Jon said, "From the way Sam is grabbing my hand, I think I can speak for both of us when I say, we would be honored."

Hope let out a sigh of relief and tears of joy as Samantha said, "This seems like a dream. Jon and I were talking yesterday about your baby. We kept saying how we hoped it would go to a good family. Then, Jon turned to me and said, 'Hey, maybe we should adopt it?' And I said, 'Yeah, maybe we should.' Then we looked at each other and realized it seemed too good to be true. But now, here we are."

Hope said, "Oh my god, you have made my world. I was so worried you would say 'no' even though in my heart, I knew you would say 'yes.'"

"Can I ask about the legality of everything?" Jon questioned.

"Well, I have talked with Jenica and she seems to think she can work it out for us. It is called a directed adoption or an identified adoption, similar to if a family member was going to adopt the baby. We are going to attempt to contact the father of the baby to obtain a waiver of paternal rights or something like that. I know it may seem like an overwhelming situation, but I am willing to go through it if you are," Hope declared.

"We are," Sam and Jon said in unison.

"Oh, I am so excited for all of you! This makes me happier than you could ever know. I have the most amazing friends. Cheers to new friends and new *unbreakable* bonds and to the little baby on the way!" I said as I raised my wine glass in the air.

"Cheers!" Everyone else exclaimed, clinking glasses and sharing hugs.

The next week was full of legal paperwork. Jenica was not kidding when she said there would be many signatures involved. Luckily, she was willing to make time for the Wilsons and Hope in the afternoons, after Hope's school day was over. Through friends, Hope was able to locate Max, the baby's biological father. He was overwhelmed, but willing to sign the waiver of paternal rights once he heard there was a good family willing to adopt. Hope, Jon, and Sam told me it would have been a much more difficult process without Jenica's help. I did not get involved in the legal part of things; however, I did continue to speak with all three of them on a daily basis. I enjoyed hearing the excitement in their voices and the love they were building for each other.

All I could think whenever we were together was how blessed this little baby was going to be. I already knew the baby would have a lot going for him or her, given Hope's personality. But, now that I knew the Wilsons would be the parents, I only believed more this baby was going to have a wonderful life. Jon and Sam continued to involve Hope in the planning for the baby, things like decorating the nursery and discussing names. Hope also made sure to keep Sam and Jon abreast of all that was happening with her. Sam told me she would occasionally get a text message from Hope that simply read, "The baby kicked me. He or she wanted to say hi to you!" Time continued to tick by, with Hope's stomach growing bigger and bigger and our excitement and anticipation rising higher and higher.

In amongst the baby planning, June 2nd was Hope's graduation day. Even with the pregnancy and all that came along with it, Hope was named the valedictorian of her class. I was valedictorian in high school, so I knew how much work it took. I was incredibly proud of her, as were Louisa and Frank, her adoptive parents. Hope invited Samantha, Jonathan, Xavier, and me to the graduation to hear her speech.

When she stood up to speak, a few gasps spread through the audience. I guessed the crowd was not expecting a five-month pregnant woman to be the one speaking. I, on the other hand, had tears in my eyes as she took the stage. The moment she began to speak, the room became mesmerized by her voice and words.

"'There is no better time than right now to be happy. Happiness is a journey, not a destination. So work like you don't need money, love like you've never been hurt, and dance like no one's watching.' I received an email from a friend a few weeks back that ended with those words. As I read them, I knew what I wanted to say to you today.

First, I want to say congratulations. We made it! But, let us not forget we still have a long way to go. We have our whole lives ahead of us. There will be peaks and valleys, but we are going to get wherever it is we are meant to be. As the email said, happiness is a journey, not a destination. May we never forget those words as our journey spreads out before us today.

Work like you don't need money. I know this may be a difficult concept for some of us. We have watched our parents struggle through bad economic conditions. Some of our parents have lost jobs, and others have worked harder than ever to barely get by. But, right now, we still have choices. Our sophomore year, we put on the play, 'You Can't Take It With You.' Let us not forget that. We do not take the money and material things with us. We are such gifted people. I only hope we can use our gifts in such a way to make a difference and find happiness along the way. Of course, we want to succeed, but may we be successful in doing something we love.

Love like you've never been hurt. Here we sit, simply teenagers. We wonder if the person we are dating is really 'the one.' Maybe he or she is. Stranger things have been known to happen. But, if not, there are so many other fish in the sea. We have all been hurt. Whether it was by a boyfriend or girl-friend or by the person we admired from afar, we have had our hearts broken, one way or another. But, we are so young. We are going to meet so many amazing people in our lives. In these past few months, I have made new friends in very unexpected places. If I had closed myself off, those friendships would not have developed. So, please, go out there and love. Love your families, love your friends, and fall in love. May we find love in our lives, love that makes the hurt worthwhile.

Dance like no one is watching. Well, this one is easy for us teenagers. We know we have done it. We have been in our rooms, or with a few friends, and that one song comes on the radio. The one song that gets our hearts pumping and just makes us want to dance. I only hope that we find experiences, people, and even songs in our lives that make us want to dance. I hope we can shine and live life to the fullest and not look behind us to see if someone is watching. May we continue to be proud to be exactly who we are right now.

So, to my dear classmates, congratulations again. I am honored to be standing here today with all of you. It has truly been an honor knowing each and every one of you. I know we will continue to make each other proud. So, as I said before, go out into the world and work like you don't need the money, love like you've never been hurt and dance like no one is watching. Congratulations!"

The room erupted in applause. The graduates whooped and hollered. Our small section had tears in our eyes as Hope returned to her seat. She looked over in our direction and waved, the smile on her face and the glow in her eyes unwavering. I had said it before and I would say it again, but I leaned in to the group around me and said, "God, she is one amazing 18-year-old."

After the graduation ceremony, Hope and her family had multiple parties to visit. So, Xavier, Jonathan, Samantha, and I said our goodbyes. I hugged Hope as tight as I could without risking the baby. I whispered in her ear, "The speech was just right. I am so very proud of you, for everything." As she walked away with her family, she turned back to us to wave. The smile and the glow were still there.

∽∾∽∾∽∾

A month later, I found myself running late to Hope's 3:30 p.m. appointment. I had been caught on a phone call at the office with a mother who believed her baby was crying because she rearranged his nursery furniture. She was calling to see if I believed altering feng shui could lead to "colic." I tried to explain colic was a condition when a baby cries for more than three hours a day with no underlying medical condition.

When I asked how long he had been crying, the mom responded, "Like 20 minutes, but all since I rearranged the furniture!" I attempted to reassure her and told her to try other common things, for instance feeding the baby or changing his diaper. I told her she could call the office again if things did not improve. She said she would, but also included in closing that she may rearrange the furniture again.

Once in my car, I drove as fast as the law would allow. This was a big appointment. It was the first the Wilsons would attend, and Lucy was planning to perform an ultrasound to determine the sex of the baby. As I made my way onto the street of Lucy's office, I found myself behind an extremely slow car. I was approaching the office, but I could not handle staying behind the slow driver, so I made a quick lane change in order to pass. I was considering sending a nasty look in their direction or possibly, for the first time in my life, using my middle finger on the road. Given my anxiety about the appointment, a few expletives did leave my mouth, including, "Who the hell are these people?"

I turned my head to the right as I passed the beige, beat-up car, and to my surprise, the car contained a group of nuns. The irony did not escape me. My years of Catholic education came rushing back, and I felt my face flush. Luckily, I had not chosen the dirty look or the finger. Instead, I smiled at the nun who was driving. I said aloud, "God, I know I may be going to hell now, but please just get me to Hope's appointment. Amen."

After recovering from the events on the road and saying a few "Hail Marys" for penance, I burst into Lucy's office at 3:35 p.m., worried I had missed the appointment. As it turned out, the waiting room was packed and Jonathan, Samantha, and Hope were sitting there talking and laughing. When she saw me, Hope waved and said, "Lucy popped her head out and said it would be a little while. I told her we were fine hanging out here. Plus, I got the text saying you were running late. You are so funny, Rose. Five minutes is not even that late. But, thanks anyways."

We continued the conversation, each full of a nervous energy awaiting the ultrasound. We wanted to make sure everything was on track and going as planned. Things seemed to be falling into place so perfectly that we were fearful if we so much as breathed the wrong way, something could go wrong. When Lucy's nurse called for Hope, we jumped out of our seats, including Jon who seemed the most nervous.

Lucy introduced herself to Jonathan and Samantha. She made them feel right at home and explained everything that would happen during the day's visit. Hope had since become more comfortable with the exam portion, so the Wilsons and I stepped out in the hall for the few minutes it took. After we returned, Lucy measured Hope's belly and listened to the baby's heartbeat. Jon and Sam had smiles on their faces and tears in their eyes when the first beat sounded. Hope caught my eye and smiled as well.

Then, it was time for the ultrasound. We huddled around the screen, as I held Hope's hand. The baby was in the right position to check anatomy. Lucy said, "Wow, this little one is going to be a model!"

First, Lucy pointed out the fingers and the toes. It was so cute to catch glimpses of each little part of the baby. At one point, the baby held its hand towards the ultrasound probe like he or she was giving us five. Lucy caught it and printed pictures for us. It was so cute, and we loved it. Then, Lucy asked, "Okay, so I am assuming everyone here wants to know the sex?"

"I am always up for sex," Jon said.

"Cute, dork. Be serious," Sam replied.

"I love you guys," Hope concluded. "And, yes, we all want to know."

"Okay, well if you look right there, you can see the legs. This is the spot you would expect to see a penis if there was one. I do not see one, but I do see what look to be perfectly forming labia. So, from what I see, you are having a little girl," Lucy stated confidently.

"Oh, Jon, a little girl," Sam said with tears in her eyes. She reached down and hugged Hope, kissing her on the cheek in the process.

"She will be perfect," I said, knowing I was speaking the truth. If she was anything like her mother or her new parents, she could not be anything but perfect.

ॐ Chapter Eighteen ॐ

It was hard to believe September had already arrived. Hope was due to deliver in the next month or so. The anxiety and excitement were palpable whenever we were together. So, when I awoke on a Saturday morning early in September, feeling slightly nauseous, I figured it was my emotions. When I vomited in the toilet, I continued to believe the same thing. I am a doctor and I should have known my own body, but the truth was, doctors made the worst patients.

It was later that same day I went to the store to buy supplies for the baby shower planned for September 15th. I was throwing the party and needed to stock up on decorations and food. I was walking through the aisles gathering items when I found myself in the "Feminine Hygiene" section. I had never really understood that terminology. They should have called it the "That Time of the Month" section or the "Men, Stay Away!" section or the "Beware Bitchy Women" section. Anyways, I was in that aisle when it hit me. In amongst all the excitement surrounding the Wilsons and Hope, I had not had my period for over a month.

I was standing there, staring at the boxes of tampons and pads, and I said, "Shit."

Sabrina looked back at me from the cart and echoed, "Shit."

"No, baby. That is not a good word to say."

"Shit," she said again. I had created a monster. I had to hope she would come up with something else to say before Xavier got home that evening. He would not be happy. So, I bribed her. I took her to the toy aisle and handed her a little stuffed puppy. I said, "Puppy."

She said, "Jakey."

I said, "Puppy."

She said, "Tuck-ew."

Good, she was happy. So, instead of buying anything else for the party, I bought a stuffed puppy and a pregnancy test. I went home and took it. Sure enough, it was positive.

When Xavier got home, I welcomed him with a glass of wine and handed him the pregnancy test. He smiled and picked me up in his arms. We had not been planning it, but it did feel pretty nice. I told him we could share the news with everyone else after the shower. I did not want to steal anyone's thunder. Things felt just right, until Sabrina ran up to Xavier and climbed in his arms. She handed him the puppy stuffed animal and said, "Shit."

"Well, where on earth did she pick that up? We really need to cut back on her television time," I said as I walked quickly upstairs.

I called Lucy to tell her about my pregnancy. She relayed her congratulations. I scheduled a piggyback appointment for myself after Hope's visit in a few weeks. First, I needed to get through the shower without a hitch.

September 15th turned out to be a lovely day. The weather was unspoiled for early fall. The leaves were changing signaling the new beginnings that were around the corner for my friends and family. I had decided to call the shower, "A Celebration of Family." People were told to come and celebrate Hope's upcoming delivery, her gift to the Wilsons, and her exciting college career, along with the new baby and the Wilsons' impending parenthood. I was sure the guests would bring gifts for Hope and for the new baby to give Sam and Jon. The menu included alcoholic and non-alcoholic beverages and an assortment of appetizers, finger foods, and sweets.

My mother and Jenica arrived early to help pre-pare the goodies. They were always better in the kitchen than I was, so I more than appreciated the help. When we were alone in the kitchen, I could not keep my mouth shut any longer. I said, "So, I do not want this to take away from today, but I am preg-nant!"

My mom immediately hugged me and began to cry. Jenica smiled and said, "That is wonderful, Rose. We will not tell anyone if you want it to stay a secret for now."

I replied, "I will likely tell Hope and Sam at some point soon because I know they will be mad if I do not. But, maybe not until after the shower, you know?"

Jenica said, "Well, we will try not to spoil the surprise. How far along are you?"

"I have been so busy lately that I cannot honestly say when my last period was, but I am guessing about ten weeks along."

"Oh, wow, you have been scattered lately if you have not noticed until now. I think you knew you were pregnant about two weeks into it with Sabrina," Jenica replied.

"I know, but it has been a good kind of scattered. The excited kind!" I said.

"Well, you know how much I had always wanted grandkids, so I am so glad you girls just keep popping them out! Now, we just need to get Kyle and Prilla engaged so they can add some to the crew," my mother said.

"No pressure, right Mom?" I asked, while hugging her.

"Of course not. I wouldn't dare," she replied with a wink.

Even though showers are traditionally for women only, this was by no means a traditional shower. My dad, Jon, Tim, Kyle, Xavier, and Frank, Hope's adoptive father, spent most of the time in the family room watching college football. I could tell Frank was glad to have the other men around to make him more comfortable. Luckily, Notre Dame was not playing that Saturday, so I was able to devote myself better to the party. Trust me; it was planned that way on purpose.

Hope and Samantha were the centers of attention in the living room. Everyone was busy asking Hope how she was feeling and about her upcoming college plans. My mother and Jenica were helping as co-hostesses. Hope's adoptive mother, Louisa, asked so many times if she could help that I finally caved in and had her organize the gifts. Jon's Aunt Geri had driven a long distance to be there with us, and she fell in love with Hope the minute she met her. Sandy, Vince, Nanny, and Poppy sent their love from Pennsylvania and, of course, gifts. A few of Hope's friends from school were able to make it, and they were fitting right in with the group.

I had asked Prilla ahead of time to take as many pictures as she could during the party. Photography was her major in college and she was currently working for a local magazine. She had met Kyle while taking pictures at the unveiling of a new airplane on which Kyle was working. After seeing an album of her pictures, Prilla had become the go-to photographer in our family. So, I knew the pictures would be gorgeous. Plus, she could spend half of her time in with the guys, around Kyle, where she really loved to be.

Mia had agreed to keep Sabrina, Brody, Brooke, and Bridget for the day. We would have loved having them there, but Jenica would not have been able to truly relax and enjoy herself if she had to run after all three of her little ones.

There was a lull in the action of the football games, so I thought it was the ideal time to open gifts. Hope seemed a bit nervous, so I walked over and whispered in her ear. "Is everything okay?"

She whispered back, "Everything is perfect. I am overwhelmed by all of this. Your family and the Wilsons have been so welcoming to me and to my parents. So, thank you."

Everyone gathered in the living room and Prilla took position to catch the gifts on film. Things got started and Hope opened her first present. It was a beautiful handmade quilt from Nanny and Poppy. She read the card aloud, "We know we have not met you, but we know we would love you. Thank you for your gift to our family. We hope this keeps you warm in your college dorm room. Love, Nanny and Poppy." A round of "Aaws" spread around the room. I saw Hope's blue eyes were already wet with tears. It was going to be an emotional day, for sure.

Next, Sam and Jon opened the gift from my parents. It was bedding and blankets for the crib, all in pink camouflage print. Jon said, "Oh my goodness, Maggie and Gerard, where did you find these?"

My mom responded, "We searched everywhere. It was actually Gerard who found a place in Canada that makes them. They seemed too good to be true."

"What a wonderful way to link the new baby to her brother, Hunter," Hope said.

"I am speechless. They are perfect. Thank you," Sam said, also fighting back tears.

It went on like that for quite awhile, each taking turns opening gifts. The time came for Hope to open the gift from Xavier and me. She ripped off the paper and a smile spread across her face when she saw what was inside - a stethoscope with her name engraved on it. I said, "I have had the pleasure of being your doctor for a few years now. And, I know you are going to be a wonderful physician someday. You mentioned you would be volunteering in a clinic when you get to the university. Well, every future physician needs a stethoscope. And, Hope, it reminds you to come home and visit every once in awhile."

"Don't worry, Rose. You will probably be sick of me. Thank you. I promise to make you guys proud."

"You already have, and you know it," I replied.

Then, Sam and Jon opened their gift from us. The first part of the gift was a little onesie with "My doctor loves me" printed on the front. "Oh, Rose, it is adorable!" Sam said.

"Hold it up!" Prilla said. "So, I can get a picture." When she did, everyone said how cute it was.

"Hey, do they make those in bigger sizes?" Hope asked.

"I did not see them, but if they do, I will get you one," I replied with a smile in her direction.

The second part of the gift was a picture frame with two openings, one with a picture of Hunter smiling in his camouflage blanket. The other was empty. The caption on the frame read, "Loves of Our Lives." Jon said, "Thank you, Rose. But, you know we are putting a picture of the baby in there and not a picture of you, right?"

"Ha-ha," I responded with a smirk. "Although I am a bit hurt, I guess I understand."

There were still more gifts to open, bringing many smiles and a few tears. At the end of the gifts, Hope said, "I have a special gift for Sam and Jon."

Sam replied, "Oh, Hope, you are giving us the biggest gift of all. You owe us nothing."

Hope said, "Just open it."

Sam read the card aloud, "Dear Sam and Jon. I could not have asked for more amazing people than you two to care for my baby. She will be in good hands, and I am so very grateful. I know we met for a reason. I know you will give her all that she deserves and more. She will be blessed to have you as parents, as I have been to have you as friends. Love, Hope."

Jon unwrapped the gift. Inside were an outfit, a blanket, and an angel stuffed animal. The clothes and blanket were embroidered with "Blessed."

Jon said, "Thank you so much, Hope. They are adorable." Sam simply hugged Hope and kissed her on the cheek.

Sam then cleared her throat and said, "We have a gift for Hope as well."

Hope opened the card and read it, "Dear Hope. You could never know the feelings we have for you. Thank you does not seem to be enough, but that is what we have to say. You have been such a joy for us, and we are honored to adopt your baby. We will do all we can to make you proud and to help her grow into a beautiful woman, just like her mother. Thank you. We hope this gift welcomes you more into our family and explains why this is so important to us. Love, Samantha and Jonathan."

Inside the package was an album with a camouflage cover and an elk engraved on the front. It was labeled, "Our Family. To Hope. Love, Jonathan and Samantha." Inside, there were pictures of Jon and Sam's wedding, then many pictures of Hunter, including some favorites of mine. I could see Hope's eyes tearing up, as she looked deep into Hunter's eyes. Next, there were pictures of all of us together. There were copies of the ultrasounds. At the end of the album were plenty of empty pages. "We hope you will fill them with the pictures we send to you through the years," Jon included.

"I would be honored to. Thank you so much. This means so much to me. And, thank you all for coming and celebrating the start of a wonderful family. And, of course, thank you to Rose for organizing the party and for bringing us together," Hope said with a smile on her face.

I said, "Well, if you really think about it, it was Hunter who brought us together. So, thank you to Hunter."

A few of the guests surrounded Hope as she looked through the album in more detail. Samantha and Jonathan told stories about each of the different pictures. One of my favorites was from their wedding day. Jon explained he had promised not to put the cake in Sam's face. Of course, he did anyways. And, Sam repaid the favor by smearing cake in his face as well. The pictures were classic. Hope said, "I would kill my future husband if he did that to me. But, I still love you, Jon, and you can still be my baby's father."

"Gee, thanks for being so forgiving," Jon replied with a smirk.

We smiled and cried through the pictures of Hunter. I could tell Hope felt even more like she was one of the family by the end of it. "You feel like family to us, but now you have the album to remind you of the family we are and the amazing little man Hunter was," Sam said.

"Well, you are family to me, too. I feel like I know Hunter through all of you and I am so blessed," Hope replied.

"That is kind of how we have felt through the years," Kyle included. "It is like we knew him."

"I only wish you all could have," Sam said with a smile hiding the tears in her eyes.

The party proved to be a success, and I was exhausted afterwards. There was a moment when only Sam, Hope, and I were sitting in the living room. I decided to take the opportunity and said, "Hey girls, I thought I should tell you. I have some news to share. I am pregnant, too. Trust me, I will let you have your moments, but I knew you would be mad if I kept it to myself too long."

They were both thrilled. They kissed me and felt my belly. We discussed how I had found out, and they loved the story about Sabrina and her newfound vocabulary word. When Jon heard I was pregnant, he also offered his congratulations and said, "Well, now, the two little ones can be best friends."

I replied, "It was one of my first thoughts when I found out. I would not want it any other way."

The upcoming weeks flew by, with doctor's appointments for Hope and me. Both of our babies were healthy, and Hope's little girl was getting ready to pop out and join the world. Hope was anxious and the Wilsons were as excited as ever. But, we seemed to be able to keep our wits about us with the support of each other.

⧉ Chapter Nineteen ⧉

I found as Hope's due date approached, I was constantly holding my cell phone and pager in my hands. I was so worried I would miss that important call or page. I was reminded of the days I did the same thing when I was concerned I would be paged that Hunter had taken a turn for the worse. Yet again, I was struck by how things had come full circle. This time, I was clutching my phone and pager with hope and excitement, whereas back then, it was with sadness and fear.

As it always seemed to happen, I was in the shower the evening of October 4th. Yes, on days off I usually took an evening shower, milking my time in pajamas as long as possible. I knew Xavier was in Brina's room playing with her, so I decided to take a longer shower and really relax. I was singing along to a country song on the radio when I heard Xavier calling for me, "Babe, you have a beautiful singing voice, but your phone just rang two times in a row. It was an unknown number. Oh, it is ringing again do you want me to pick up?"

"Oh my god! It could be Hope. Yes, pick up!" I yelled as I finished rinsing and quickly climbed out of the shower.

I overheard Xavier saying, "Hi...Yes, take a deep breath...Okay, I will tell her...We are on our way...We will call them, too...Yes, just take care of yourself...See you soon."

"Aaah!" I screamed. "Was it Hope?"

"Yes, her water broke not too long ago and she is having increasing contractions. She called Lucy and is now waiting for an ambulance to take her to the hospital."

"An ambulance! Why? Is everything okay?"

"Yes, Rose, everything is okay. She is by herself and did not feel like driving amid contractions. She is a smart girl, remember?"

As I threw on clothes and ran a comb through my hair, I asked Xavier if he would drive me. He replied, "Of course. I would not trust you to be able to find the hospital in your current state."

"Ha-ha. Very funny. I have driven to and from the hospital in worse states than this and you know it! Could you get Brina strapped into the car?"

"Yes, dear. And, you can call the Wilsons while we are on our way."

"Right, the Wilsons. That would be important. Okay. Even better you will be driving," I said, realizing I was more nervous for Hope than I had been when I went into labor with Sabrina.

I was already dialing Samantha's cell phone as I climbed into the passenger seat of Xavier's silver Lexus. She picked up after one ring, "Hello?"

"Sam, it's Rose. Hope is in labor. Get your asses to the hospital STAT!"

"Wow, hello to you, too. You better clean up that language before the baby comes," Sam responded sarcastically.

"I know when I can use it and when I cannot. Sabrina has learned to tune me out when I am in a tizzy."

"She didn't the other day," Xavier said under his breath.

I shot him a look out of the corner of my eye as Sam said, "Well, Jon is out in the yard. We will get changed and be there as fast as we can. Keep us posted. Take a deep breath, honey. We don't need two pregnant ladies in labor today, okay?"

"I will. I think once I am there with her, I will be able to relax a bit. X! The light was yellow! You could have gone! Why did you stop?"

Sam replied from the other end of the phone, "That's my Rose. Please don't kill Xavier on the way there. We will need you both. See you soon."

I hung up the phone and looked over at Xavier. He did not look too amused. "Rose, we are still going to beat the ambulance by at least ten minutes, so please, sit there and relax."

"You know I hate the word 'relax.'" I said.

"Well, relax anyways."

Xavier proved to be right. When I ran into the ER, flashing my doctor badge and asking to see Hope Shields, they told me she was still en route in the ambulance. Okay, I could finally calm down a little.

My phone rang and I picked it up within a second. I said, "Hope?"

"No, it is your mother."

"Oh, sorry, Mom. Hope is in labor. We just got to the hospital."

"I know. Xavier called me while parking the car. He asked if your father and I could come and pick up Sabrina."

"God, how does he keep his head on so straight at a time like this?"

My mother continued, "We are getting ready right now and should be leaving in about five minutes. Do you need us to bring anything, like maybe a sedative for you?"

"Very funny, Mom, but, no, I cannot think of anything."

"Okay. I am assuming we should meet you on the Labor and Delivery floor?"

"Yeah, by the time you get here, we will likely have moved up there. Say you are here for Hope Shields. Oh, Mom, Lucy is walking up to me. I am going to get the update. See you when you get here. Thanks. Love you."

"Love you, too," she said as I was hanging up.

I hugged Lucy as she said, "Sounds like today is the big day. Are Samantha and Jonathan on their way too?"

"Yes. They should be here within a half hour. How close together were her contractions when she called you?"

"Four to five minutes, so she was getting really anxious but said the pain was not terrible. The ambulance just checked in with an ETA of five minutes, so let's head up to the Labor and Delivery floor. I gave them directions to get her vitals and roll her right up there."

Just then, Xavier walked in with Sabrina and all her things in tow. He also hugged Lucy. When she laid eyes on Sabrina, Lucy smiled the biggest smile I had seen on her face in awhile. "Aren't you the most darling thing I have ever seen?"

Sabrina replied, "Yeah."

"She is humble," I said through my laughter.

We trekked up to the Obstetrics floor, getting Xavier a visitor badge along the way. Xavier set up camp with Sabrina in the waiting room, while Lucy and I went in to what would be Hope's delivery room. It was only a few minutes later that Hope came along in a wheelchair. Somehow, she managed to still look beautiful, even in the throes of labor. I ran to her and gave her a huge hug. She said, "My God, Rose. You look like shit. I am the one in labor here."

"Gee, nice to see you too, dear," I replied. With that, I looked in the mirror and realized she was right.

I helped Hope to get situated and then said, "Well, now that you are here, I can calm down. So, give me a minute to clean myself up."

I took a few minutes in the bathroom, brushed my hair, and threw on some lip-gloss and mascara. There were likely going to be pictures taken and I refused to look like I had been run over by a truck. When I came back in the room, my parents, Xavier, and Sabrina were there. Hope was comfortable on the bed. My mom was saying, "You are almost there, Hope. You are going to do great!"

"Mom, Dad, wow, you made it in record timing. Thank you so much for coming!" I said while hugging them both.

"As much as we would love to stay, I think it would be better if we got Sabrina out of your hair. We will plan on keeping her tonight, since it is already getting late."

"Thank you both," Xavier said. "That way, I can be of help around here as much as I am able."

"Okay, well, Sabrina, come to Granny, sweetie." Sabrina jumped in my mother's arms with excitement in her eyes. "Hope, we will be praying for you and the little one. Good luck. See you sometime tomorrow, okay?"

"Sounds good. Thanks for everything," Hope replied.

"Bye, Hope. Everything's going to go great," my dad said, never one for emotional moments. Brina included, "Bye Hopie. C'mon Gwandpap." They left the room, leaving us standing around Hope's bed.

I was about to ask if Hope needed anything when her blue eyes clouded over. "Oh no, a contraction is coming again. Hold my hand, Rose."

"Got it covered," I replied as I let her squeeze my hand. "Wow, girl, you are strong."

"So are these contractions. Whew. I apologize ahead of time for any bad language that might escape my lips. Okay, that one is over. Tell Lucy it was about four minutes from the last one. I hope Sam and Jon are close-by."

"They should be rolling in really soon," I said just as Lucy returned with Jon and Sam right behind her. "Well, speak of the devils."

Sam was holding an adorable teddy bear that had "Thank You" stitched across its chest. "This is for you, Hope."

"Oh, to think this started with a teddy graham on the ultrasound, and now I am getting a big teddy bear. It seems quite fitting. Thank you."

Both Jon and Sam leaned in to kiss Hope on the cheek. She seemed to relax a little, knowing they were there. I kissed them both, too, asking if they were ready.

"I am. It is hard to believe the time is here," Sam said, sounding a bit nervous.

"I was born ready," Hope said from the bed, with a big smile on her face.

"That is what I like to hear," Jon said. "Sam was a whiner when Hunter was born. I bet you won't even make a peep."

"Well, no promises there. The contractions are already pretty painful. But, I will try to stay strong," Hope said.

"I am kidding. You can scream all you want. I don't even want to imagine the pain," Jon replied, trying to be supportive.

"Yeah, tell me about it. I cannot even fathom what it feels like," Xavier said.

"Spoken like true men," Lucy concluded.

Another contraction came on right about then, and Xavier and Jon each took a hand. "Wow, you *can* squeeze!" Xavier said.

"Okay, darling, we are going to get you hooked up to the fetal monitors. These contractions are getting closer together now. Are your parents coming?" Lucy asked.

"Louisa, my mom, is on her way. Frank has to stay at home with the other kids. There is no one else who can really be there to take care of them overnight, so he will try to get here tomorrow."

In between contractions, Samantha sat on the bed next to Hope and pulled a piece of folded paper out of her pocket. She said to Hope, "We decided on a name and we want to make sure you approve."

In true "Hope-fashion," she replied, "Approve? You could name her ESPN or Karma or any of the other strange names I have heard recently. I would still know I made the right decision by choosing you."

"Trust me, it is more likely Jon would want her named NASCAR, but you do not have to worry," Sam said.

"Wait, I could name her NASCAR? That's it, I change my vote," Jon said matter-of-factly.

Sam continued, "Umm, let me think, no. So, Hope, I wanted you to know why we chose this name. I came across this poem on one of the adoption websites. When I shared my idea with Jonathan, he loved it, too. That is, of course, until he realized NASCAR was an option. The poem reads,

'Do you know you are my angel?

Do you know I love you so?
You are not of my blood, not of my womb.
You are a gift, given to me by another.
But, I love you, angel, as if you are my own.'

So, if you approve, we would like to name her Angel Hope Wilson."

Jon said, "Plus, you gave us the angel stuffed animal. So, we figured, in a way, you helped pick the name, too."

I immediately saw the dampness in Hope's eyes as the biggest smile crossed her face. "I love it. It is completely perfect. And, thank you for including Hope in her name. It means the world to me."

"Well, you and Angel mean the world to us," Jon interjected.

"And, what am I, chopped liver?" I asked from the corner with a chuckle.

"Oh, Rose, stop being a dork. We love you too and you know it," Hope said from her bed. We laughed as I walked over and kissed her forehead.

"Plus, that makes my tattoo an easy decision. I will get a small angel tattoo," Hope said. I quickly realized I had forgotten to talk her out of it.

Just then, another contraction began and I was in the right place to hold her hand. At that moment, Louisa came running in the room. Hope lit up when she saw her. Louisa hugged and kissed Hope, then passed hugs around the room. She was tearful, but I could also tell she was very proud of how Hope was handling the situation. "Frank sends his love, sweetie."

"I know. He called earlier with the same message. Are the other kids okay?" Hope replied.

"They are all fine. Saying prayers, of course."

We tried to pass the time between contractions with funny stories and anecdotes. Hope had a smile on her face the entire time. Even when a contraction broke her concentration, she had enough spunk to make a joke. During one exceptionally painful one, she said, "I may be going through this pain, but Sam and Jon, you are the ones who are going to have to deal with the pain of raising a teenage girl someday. Trust me when I say - we girls are not easy!"

"Tell me about it, but I can honestly say it was worth it," Louisa said while holding Hope's hand.

The contractions were moving closer and closer together and we waited with bated breath for Lucy to say it was time to push. It seemed to be forever, but Lucy finally announced it was time. Xavier stepped out in the hall to give Hope privacy, but Jon decided to stay with Hope's approval. It was crowded, and the delivery room was more than full of love for Hope and the baby about to enter the world.

When Hope started to push, I coached her, as we had learned in class. As if I ever doubted her, she was a trouper. She screamed a little and perhaps uttered a swear word or two, but all in all, she was the picture of grace. Sam said, "I cannot believe it, but in a way, I knew it. You even look spectacular while in labor. It is so not fair." That comment lit up Hope's eyes and I knew she would have smiled if she were not pursing her lips while pushing.

Then, Lucy called for one last push. Hope strained and screamed, and then, the most delightful sound emerged – Angel began to cry. Lucy lifted the baby up for us to see, and then handed her to the nurses. They cleaned her off quickly and wrapped her in a pink blanket. Lucy picked Angel up in her arms and looked to Samantha who pointed to Hope. Lucy nodded in understanding and placed Angel on Hope's chest. We were tearful in that moment, but Hope was finally able to let out her own tears. She reached around Angel and stared into her eyes. She said, "Sam, it is just like you told me it would be. It was worth it for this moment. And, it was worth it to know I am giving you the biggest gift of all."

Samantha and Jonathan responded, "Thank you." It seemed the perfect and only thing that needed to be said. We gathered around Hope and Angel. Xavier came back in the room and gave Hope a kiss on the forehead. We took turns kissing Hope and Angel and giving our love and congratulations to Hope, Samantha, and Jonathan. I caught Jon's eye and we shared a knowing glance. We were linked around a hospital bed, similar to the moment when Hunter passed away. But, now, we were gathered together in hope for the future. We had been through so much to reach this moment, coming full circle.

୬ Chapter Twenty ଡ଼

While Hope was holding Angel in her arms, the clock ticked past midnight. "You missed having a different birthday by only a few minutes, baby," she said to Angel.

Lucy was busy delivering the placenta and all the non-glorified parts of the birth process. She was pointing out important tidbits to her resident as she went along. I was reminded of my medical student rotation on the Obstetrics service. The birth of a baby was always a precious event, but the placenta was another story altogether. It was better most new mothers were too engulfed in their newborns to notice. Hope was no different, completely mesmerized by our new little Angel.

"Okay, I have had my moment or two. It is time for..." Hope paused in the middle of her sentence and caught her breath. "Whew, sorry about that. It is time for Angel to be held by her wonderful parents, Sam and Jon."

"Well, you know you will always be her birth mother, Hope," Sam replied, "and that will never change."

"I know. But, you..." Another pause. Another catch of her breath. I figured she was overwhelmed with emotion surrounding the situation. "You should hold her, Sam and Jon. This is your moment, too."

Sam took Angel into her arms and both Sam and Jon began to cry. They were not the only ones; we joined in with them.

"Hello, beautiful Angel. We love you very much," Sam whispered. We were focused on the baby when Hope said, "Umm, Rose, I feel funny, like I cannot catch my breath. What is going on?"

Immediately, Lucy stood up and came to Hope's side, leaving the resident to finish up. She took her stethoscope and listened to Hope's lungs. "You are breathing really fast. Rose, hook up the saturation monitor to her finger, please."

I did what I was told, but I could read fear in Lucy's eyes as the saturation monitor read 88%. Louisa asked, "What is wrong?"

Hope said, "I am scared. My chest really hurts. Maybe I am just anxious, but it sure feels different."

I tried to reassure her, saying, "Hope, stay strong, sweetie. We are here for you. Let us know what you..."

Before I could complete my statement, all hell broke loose. Angel began to cry, with Sam and Jon attempting to comfort her. I had never heard a sadder cry. It was as if she was feeling her mother's anxiety. In that same moment, Hope's arms clenched and her eyes rolled back in her head. She began shaking violently. I was frozen. I had dealt with similar situations at the hospital before, but I found myself in disbelief. This could not be happening, not to my Hope.

"She is having a seizure. Xavier, pull down that button on the wall that says 'Code Blue,'" Lucy yelled, though still appearing in control of her emotions.

Xavier did as he was told as I put an oxygen mask on Hope's stunning face, believing it would make a difference. Lucy said, "Push two milligrams of Ativan now." A nurse came running in with the medication and gave it through Hope's IV. That appeared to stop the seizure, but even with the oxygen mask, Hope was only saturating 85 out of 100%. She was not getting enough oxygen and I was very concerned. I could only think of a few conditions that would cause Hope's symptoms and I was not reassured by the thought of any of them.

The code team descended around Hope with tools to intubate her and help her breathe. I trusted them and had faith they would be able to do more for her.

The fog of Hope's seizure seemed to pass for barely a second, maybe with the help of the Ativan. Hope looked first at me. Then, she searched the room until her eyes fell on Angel. She looked at Sam, Jon, and Angel, who were standing together crying. Hope was trying to say something. I leaned in close, moving people out of the way, trying to make out her words. She simply said, "Love her."

As the words left her mouth, the monitors began to beep uncontrollably. My mind was running rampant. This could not be happening. Things were moving too quickly. Hope's oxygen saturation was down to 65% and her heart rate was not picking up on the tracing. I realized I was crying without even knowing it. Tears were pouring down my face, but I knew I needed to help.

Lucy said, "We need to start CPR. Who can do chest compressions?"

I climbed up on the bed, wanting to hug Hope in my arms, but instead, I began compressions. I started counting out thrusts as the respiratory therapist was giving Hope breaths with an oxygen bag. I looked up long enough to see Louisa standing in Xavier's arms. Everyone in the room was crying, yet still doing everything to save Hope.

One nurse was drawing blood, an anesthesiologist was placing a tube down Hope's throat, and another nurse was drawing up medications as Lucy yelled them out. I was trying to get a rhythm on the heart monitor. I kept looking up, hoping to see something. Another physician asked if I needed a break. I simply shook my head. This was my job as Hope's doctor and I did not feel tired.

This scene continued for an unknown amount of time. My arms began to burn, but I would not give up. I would not allow myself to look in Hope's eyes, because I already knew the sparkle was gone, and with it, my heart was breaking. The code team was breathing for her through the endotracheal tube, but she was still not getting the oxygen she needed. I was pushing on her chest, but her heart was not beating. Lucy finally had to pull me away with great effort.

Lucy held me in her arms as I cried. She whispered, "She did an amazing thing today. I am so very sorry." Then she announced to everyone present, "I am so sorry. She is gone."

I looked up and saw Samantha, tears streaming down her cheeks, walking over to Hope's bed. Hope was connected to monitors and had multiple lines attached to her, but Sam took Angel, who was still wailing, and laid her on Hope's chest. It was in that moment Angel finally stopped crying, which only made us sob. Hope looked beautiful lying there with her precious daughter in her arms. It seemed so unfair. She was likely the most selfless 18-year-old in the world, and yet, she was taken from us. It had gone so quickly, but looking at the clock, I realized how much time had in reality passed.

I needed to leave the room to clear my head, but something held me there. I walked up to Hope's body, kissed her on the cheek, and whispered, "I love you so much. You will be missed, Hope. You will live on in that adorable little girl. She is in good hands."

Angel remained quiet, sleeping peacefully as tubes and lines were removed from Hope's body. It seemed surreal. The girl who had been so strong throughout her pregnancy, throughout her life, was no longer there. We hugged each other as we cried. Louisa said she had to call Frank, as she stepped out in the hall. I stood there, with Xavier's arms around me, not knowing what to say or what to do. Out of nowhere, Angel began to cry. Lucy said, "She might be hungry. Sam, you should be the one to feed her."

The nurse handed Samantha a bottle of formula. As she picked Angel up off Hope's chest, Sam could not stop her own tears. But, just by holding her, Sam was able to curb Angel's crying. Samantha held the beautiful baby tight in her arms and fed her the bottle. Jon kept his arms around both of them for the entire feeding. It was such a breathtaking sight. They made a lovely family. I knew Angel would be okay, but I also knew she would grow up learning about her mother and the sacrifices Hope made for her.

Hope's black hair spread out around her lovely face as she lay there. I could not believe how much she looked like she was asleep. It was the same as when Hunter died. I really expected her to open her dark blue eyes and make a joke, but the joke did not come. I missed her so much already. The nurses moved us into one of the family rooms, so we could be together. We each took turns going in to say our good-byes to Hope.

While waiting, we passed Angel around, giving her as many kisses and as much love as were humanly possible. I knew I would not let Angel go a day without knowing how much Hope loved her from the moment she was conceived. She would be a testament to the amazing person Hope was and was meant to be but never got the chance. Although, I have to say, for an 18-year-old, she had touched a great amount of people, as Hunter had in his 11 months.

Lucy joined us in the family room at one point with tears in her eyes. She said, "I just received some of the labs that were drawn. I know this is going to be a lot of medical information, but I also realize you must have many questions. Hope had severe clotting issues with her blood, likely caused by something called disseminated intravascular coagulation. Those lab results, along with her symptoms, lead me to believe she likely passed from an amniotic fluid embolism. Unfortunately, we do not know a lot about this condition. We think some of the amniotic fluid enters the mother's circulation and causes an inflammatory process that clots off the vessels to her lungs. The mother's lungs cannot get the blood they need, so air exchange does not happen. Then the whole process leads to heart failure and cardiac arrest. Unfortunately, supportive care is all we can do, and studies show that 80% of mothers will likely die if they suffer from an amniotic fluid embolism. I am so sorry for all of you. I loved her, too. We will have more answers later, but I am here if any of you have questions now."

My mind was reeling. I could remember learning about amniotic fluid emboli. They were extremely rare, so why Hope? The most important thing I recalled was the emboli presented suddenly, with no preceding symptoms. There was no sure way to know a patient was at risk. It was what made the condition so frightening. Beyond supportive measures, there was nothing more to do. Most patients died even with the most extreme measures taken. We caught it early. We had done everything by the book, and yet, we still lost her. Some mothers suffered from amniotic fluid emboli during the delivery, which also put the baby at risk. Thank God, Angel had been delivered safely although Hope was still gone. I could not seem to get my mind around that fact.

"I wanted her to be here with us," Sam interrupted my thoughts and said quietly from next to me.

"I know you did," I replied.

"I really wanted Angel to know her. I never wanted this."

"I know, Sam. Do not even think that way. You loved her, too."

"I really did. I never imagined I would be going through this without her, actually," Sam said through more tears.

"Well, we are all here with you. We are not going anywhere. You know how loved Hunter was. Angel is not going to be any different, okay?" I said with as much resolve as I could muster in that moment.

"Thank you, Rose," she said as she stood up to say her good-bye to Hope, taking Angel with her.

I called my parents while Samantha was in with Hope. It was so hard to give them the news. It was bittersweet. "Angel is breathtaking, but Hope passed away." At least the two events happened on two different dates, so Angel would still have a birthday to celebrate without it being the exact anniversary of Hope's death. My parents were as supportive as ever. They said they would keep Sabrina as long as was necessary. I thanked them, but said they were our first stop after leaving the hospital. I also called Jenica and Kyle who had gotten to know Hope during this process. They were both heart-broken, as were we all. Kyle was watching Tucker and Jake at our house, so I told him we would not be back until later. He told me to take all the time we needed. I noticed Xavier was close-by the whole time, in case I needed him at any moment.

When my turn to say good-bye arrived, I walked into Hope's room, unable to believe I had to say my final words to her. I had a hard time speaking, but I knew I had a few things to say. I simply spoke, "Hope, we will love her. I promise we will. You can rest knowing she is loved. As you were loved. I will miss you dearly. God bless you. Tell Hunter hello for me. I love you." I kissed her one last time on the cheek, squeezed her hand, and left the room.

ç Christmas Eve continued ç

ç Chapter Twenty-one ç

My eyes are still fixated on the pictures of Hunter and Hope on the mantle when Jenica walks up behind me and says, "Hey. Where did you go? You have been dazing for the last few minutes."

It is only then I realize I am crying. I quickly wipe my eyes as I turn to look at Jenica. She notices the gesture and asks, "My goodness, Rose, are you okay?"

I reply, "Yes, yes. Just emotional, I guess. Must be the pregnancy hormones. As if being a fatty wasn't enough."

It is then Kyle begins to clink his glass with a spoon. I am hopeful he will take the attention away from my sappy tears. I do not want to ruin the festive mood. Before Kyle has a chance to talk though, Jon catches my eye. He always has a way of reading my emotions, even when I try to hide them. I wink and smile, letting him know I am okay.

Kyle starts with a bit of a shake in his voice, "So, you know how much I love speaking in front of people. I cannot even order a pizza without getting nervous, so bear with me. First, I want to say 'thank you' to Xavier and Rose for having us over tonight. The house looks terrific, you guys." Jake and Tucker walk up at that moment and start licking Kyle's leg.

"Oh yes, sorry, 'thank you' to Jake and Tucker, too. And Brina, of course. That said, I have an announcement."

"You are pregnant!" I say in the most sarcastic voice I can find. Everyone laughs. My dad says, "Come on, Rose." So, some things never change.

Kyle continues. "Well, that is it. Rose blew it. Thanks a lot. No seriously, though. I wanted to tell you while we are together. A miracle happened today. Prilla agreed to marry me!"

There is a round of cheering in the room. My mom's eyes fill with tears, although I have the sense she knew before and actually kept the secret. My dad smiles and appears quite proud.

It is then I realize Prilla is still in her coat and gloves, although she took her hat off. "You sneaky girl! You are covering your ring with the gloves," I say.

She proudly removes her gloves and holds out her left hand. All the girls in the room run to look at it. The ring is a solitaire diamond, princess cut, on a simple platinum band. It fits Prilla perfectly. "Nice job, Kyle. It is beautiful," Jenica says.

"How did you ask her?" Xavier asks over the heads of all the women gawking at the ring.

"Well, if the girls can control themselves for a moment, I will let Prilla tell the story," Kyle replies.

Prilla begins with a smile on her face, "Kyle asked if I wanted to go and watch the planes take off and land at the airport. You may think this is an odd request, but it happens to be very romantic. We actually do it quite often. It is how I get him to agree to see chick-flicks. We compromise."

She continues, "So, we were sitting out by the runway, and Kyle told me to look over at the baggage claim truck near the Southwest gates. When I did, I realized there was something written on the side of the truck. I could not believe my eyes. It said, 'Prilla, will you marry me?' In that moment, I turned to Kyle with tears in my eyes. He kind of fumbled to open the ring box, which was so cute." I look at Kyle and we catch each other's eyes and smile. I have always made fun of Kyle for his awkward hands, but it makes him even that much more endearing.

Kyle interjects, "One of my friends is working in the baggage claim department, so I had a connection."

"Yes, he got lucky. Well, in more ways than one actually, right, Kyle?" Prilla says.

"Right, honey," Kyle responds with a smile.

"Then, he told me all the reasons he loves me. By that point, I was crying. And, he asked me if I would marry him. Of course, I said 'yes.' The moment, the ring, the airport, and everything else were better than I could have imagined," Prilla concludes.

"At least I said more than, 'Will you marry me?' Right, Xavier?" Kyle jokes while looking over at Xavier and me.

Xavier responds, "Under the Golden Gate Bridge, Kyle. Enough said."

I kiss Xavier on the cheek as I say, "It was perfect for me, honey. Do not listen to him."

I walk over to Kyle and Prilla again and engulf them in a huge pregnant hug. Just then, the baby kicks in my stomach. I say, "Well, the little one is happy. He or she just kicked the hell out of my uterus."

Sabrina flies across the room and yells, "Wanna feel, Mommy!"

As Brina grabs my belly, the hugs and congratulations pass around the room. We have been waiting for this. Prilla walks up and whispers in my ear, "You girls did well. I always say I am glad I met a man with two older sisters."

I kiss her on the cheek as the room begins to quiet down. I decide to follow up Kyle's announcement with one of my own. I am able to get Xavier's attention first and he joins me in front of the Christmas tree.

Gil says in a loud voice, "Wait, we already know you are pregnant! And, my science knowledge may not be great, but I do not think you can get pregnant again on top of the baby already in your stomach. Then again, you are the doctor!"

"Keep drinking, Gil," Xavier replies amid more laughter. What a fabulous Christmas Eve this has become.

The tears are already stinging my eyes as I begin to speak, "Xavier and I had my checkup appointment this week. We had an ultrasound done. And, yes, Gil, there is only one baby. I could not handle triplets like you, Jenica. The big news is that it is going to be a little boy!"

"Yes!" Brody yells from Tim's lap. We turn his way. He responds to this by saying, "Too many girls!"

I continue, "We have kept it a secret for the last few days, but we did already tell Jon and Sam. We wanted to ask them a very important question. We asked whether we could have the honor of giving the baby Hunter as his middle name. And, they said, 'yes.'" With that, most eyes in the room were wet with tears, especially those of Jon and Sam.

"So, although most of you never had the privilege of meeting Hunter, I think you feel as though you knew him. He was a beautiful, perfect, little man. We could only hope and pray for as much in our little guy. I wanted to take this time to share the news with all of you and to say, from the bottom of our hearts, 'thank you!'"

Jon and Sam walk up to us, with Angel smiling in Jon's arms, and we share a family-sized embrace. Hugs and kisses again are passed around the room. The magic of Christmas is almost palpable. In true holiday spirit, at that very moment, my dad announces, "Look everybody, it is snowing." There has been snow on the ground, but it has not snowed in a few days. It is dazzling, so we pause for a moment and look out the window. Brooke screams, "Let's build a snowman!"

Jenica says, "We need to eat first, Brooke, honey. Maybe after dinner, okay?"

I clink my glass one more time. A hush comes over the room again. "Come on, I am going to need to go get more Kleenex if there are going to be more emotional announcements," my mom complains with a smile on her face.

I say, "Hopefully this is not too sad. I would like to make a toast, with my non-alcoholic beverage of course. First, I would like to toast Xavier. At Christmas, I only realize even more how much I love you. When my hormones are running high and you still find me beautiful, it keeps me going. Thank you." Everyone clinks his or her glasses and drinks.

"To the little ones, Sabrina, Brody, Brooke, and Bridget. You really remind us of what Christmas is all about. Your smiles and the shining in your eyes should be bottled up and sold. We would be millionaires. And, to the tiny one in my belly, we cannot wait for your smiles and bright eyes, either! I love you all."

"Cheews, Mommy," Brina says to me with her sippy cup of apple juice.

"To my brother-in-law Jack, and our pups, Tucker and Jake. Thank you for being here and for avoiding the Christmas tree this year!" A round of laughter and glass tapping follows.

"Wow, come on, Rose. Yours may be non-alcoholic, but ours are real!" Gil says.

"On that note, to you Gil. And to Mindy. Thank you for coming. In this house, friends are family. We hope you know that."

"To my in-laws Mom and Dad Gorman, who are likely spending a warm night on the beach, while we are here in the snow. We wish you could be here. We love you both."

"To my sister-in-law Melony. It means a lot that you drove tonight in this weather. We are looking forward to celebrating again with you and your parents in California in a week!"

"Thank you, Rose. Xavier, shouldn't you also toast your beautiful wife and sister?"

"It is Rose's moment, Melony."

"More like 30 minutes," Tim says.

"I'm pregnant, not deaf, Tim. Okay, I will hurry up. Long story short."

"Too late," Kyle and Jenica say in unison, an inside joke among the siblings.

"To Kyle and Prilla. I could not be happier. Kyle, I knew you would wait until you found perfection, and you did. Prilla, welcome to the family. I love you both."

"To Jenica and Tim. Seeing you do such a fabulous job raising the triplets helps me believe we can do even half that with our own children. Sabrina and our little guy, Hunter's namesake, are blessed to have your kids and you both to look up to! I love you." Wow, everyone is starting to look a little tipsy, but I know I can finish quickly.

"To my parents. None of this is possible without you. I hope you look around this room with as much pride and love as I do. We owe it to you. You taught us throughout our lives family is not just about blood. It is about love. Thank you. I love you more than you could ever know." My mom is crying now, and pulling more tissue out of her purse. My dad is reading the TV guide, but he does look up and smile at me.

"To Samantha and Jonathan. I love you both. You know that. I cannot thank you enough for the blessing of having been Hunter's doctor. You shared your precious boy with me. You shared your lives with me. We are family, now. And, I am grateful every single day. You have made my life better. And, to our little Angel, you are such a blessing. You have brightened our lives. Your eyes carry the sparkle of your beautiful mother, Hope, and your brother, Hunter. Please know how loved you are. Cheers to the Wilsons." More clinking, more tears.

As I begin the final toast, I glance down at my right foot in its black strappy sandal. Tears fill my eyes as I focus on the two hearts side by side, one hunter green and one the dark blue of Hope's eyes. I look up again at my friends and family as I say, "And, last but not least, to Hunter and Hope. God, I really wish you could both be here. I know you are looking down, smiling at these amazing people joined here tonight. No matter how happy I am, though, I miss you tremendously. You are our angels. I am a better person because of you both. Your spirits are always with us. I know that. We all know that. Without you, we would not be here together. So, above all, thank you. We all miss you and we all love you. To Hunter and Hope!"

By now, the tears are flowing. But, in a way, they are more tears of happiness. There is a feeling in the room - an overall sense of love. I know in my heart Hunter and Hope are sharing the moment with us. I will never stop missing them. There will likely not be a day that goes by when I do not have a thought of one or both of them. Whether it is in the eyes – those of Sabrina, a patient, or a baby in the grocery store line - or in the smiles – those of Angel, our new little boy, or an infant in front of me at church - my heart will feel a little happier as I am reminded of my angels, Hunter and Hope, and all the blessings I have in my life.

So, have you looked? Have you seen them? Did I not tell you that the eyes and the smiles matter more than you could have ever imagined?

Made in United States
Orlando, FL
16 September 2023

37009958R00137